INTOLERANCE

INTOLERANCE

BY BRIAN OXLEY

PUBLISHED BY
EMBLEM MEDIA

AUTHOR
Brian Oxley

EDITORS
Greg Bandy
Steve Bumpas
Lon Lucieer

ILLUSTRATOR
Tim Ladwig

DESIGN
Erik Peterson

SPECIAL THANKS
Sally Oxley, my wife

ISBN **978 1 9410012 04 8**

Library of Congress Control Number: 2014938609

Published by Emblem Media, LLC
505 Periwinkle Ct., Ft. Myers, FL 33908

Find us at: **www.emblemmediallc.com**

Contents

To Sally, my wife, my friend, my lover...

Our two hearts beat as one. Often, when I am weary, and my strength fails me, your heart beats for the two of us.

At times I have pursued greatness, yet my heart remained in torment—for I could find neither greatness nor peace of mind. Yet you—you, who never sought greatness, simply stood there, waiting with a smile that said, "All is forgiven."

You taught me about God's love: His forgiveness of sin, and the pain He bore for us.

Whenever I awake early in the morning and, reaching out for you, find you not there, I am comforted in the knowledge that you are spending time with Him.

God has blessed our lives with three wonderful daughters, their husbands and many grandchildren. Our hearts beat all the stronger now, for there are so many more to love.

Together, we must continue to pray that His love will likewise beat in their hearts.

God gives us His Word, and He comforts us, so we know that when the day comes that our hearts cease to beat, His heart will continue to beat in all His own children and for the rest of the world's children.

Foreword

The death of a parent can be one of the most devastating events we endure. The pain and grief are often accompanied by tough questions about our life, our destiny and our fragile mortality. Lurking in our hearts is a disconcerting reminder that we all have a rendezvous with a six-foot hole in the ground. Such events invite more specific questions: "What really matters at the end? Where are we going? Why are we here?"

When my father died after a long battle with Alzheimer's disease, I was faced with some serious life questions—those same questions which grieve many after losing a parent. I was the beneficiary of a great dad, whose sacrifice, support and wisdom helped set me on the right path. I wondered... "What really matters now? Where is our culture heading? And what can I do about it?" This book is part of my pilgrimage to seek answers to the imposing questions concerning the meaning of life and the current path mapped out for society.

Why choose a fictional story to deal with such real-life questions? Well, as C. S. Lewis once wrote, "Reason is the natural order of truth; but imagination is the organ of meaning." Sometimes, fiction is just the best way to communicate the reality of non-fiction.

By now (that is, if you've read this far) you might be asking, "OK, so what is *this* story about?" As a starting point, imagine a world controlled by technology. You laugh, of course, at this "premise," saying this certainly doesn't require a great stretch of the imagination. But may I respond by asking in return whether anyone *really* understands how much of our daily life is completely controlled by sophisticated technology? Humans realized long ago that technology could provide them with the superiority they craved....

In the ancient Old Testament book of Genesis, we are told of a city with an amazing tower. The story claims that, at that time, all the people on earth spoke a single language. Some scholars think the ancient warrior King Nimrod may have commissioned the famous tower for this city. The people there wanted to make a name for themselves, to control their destiny on their own terms. It must have been quite an architectural achievement, because the story claims that God Himself came down to earth to observe.

God's conclusion was that the tower portended all kinds of troublesome possibilities for the human race, because it revealed that *if* they could do this, *nothing* would be impossible for man. And what was God Almighty's solution? Confuse them with all kinds of different languages, hence the term "babel." The biblical text ends by explaining that this confusion of languages resulted in the scattering of the existing population abroad.

Fast-forward to today with the obvious realization that man never really stopped building monuments—pyramids, temples, skyscrapers and towers. And today, nations continue to compete in a race to build the tallest tower, vainly trying to make a name for themselves. But the most impressive tower being built today is far more colossal than anything the builders of Babylon could ever imagine. And just because we don't see it, doesn't mean it doesn't exist.

Where is this tower, you ask? Well, let's start by answering some questions. When you woke up today, how many minutes passed before you gazed at some electronic screen? Or was it only a matter of seconds? Each morning you probably enjoy the convenience of refrigerated or heated food for breakfast. All the electrical power required for activating a digital screen or maintaining your food's temperature is controlled, ultimately, by software. Now, keep going... Consider the impact of transportation, telecommunications, banking systems, health networks, military defense, industrial logistics, retail inventory, governmental operations, etc., on your life. All these entities run on software. Computers, ultimately, rely on a simple universal language of ones and zeroes. So when you think about it...are we all speaking the same language again, as in the ancient days before the biblical Tower of Babel?

Despite the amazing advances in technology and standards of living, today's civilization agonizes in the upheaval of opposing worldviews. We survive somewhere in the dangerous tension between anarchy and totalitarianism. If you doubt this, observe what happens in urban centers in the midst of riots or the aftermath of natural disasters. The precariously thin blue line of government (and law enforcement) is all that stands between humane society and murderous mob rule. The pendulum of history leans back and forth between lawlessness and total control. This is nothing new...it's happened before, and it's going to happen again. But here's what will be different in the near future. No government, no totalitarian regime has ever had the supernatural power of computerized machines to control human beings. Until now, kings and despots have had to rely on a certain amount of "strength in numbers" willing to ruthlessly bear the iron force of weapons and rule upon a citizenry. The system only worked if a large group of human enforcers were convinced of its benefits and were willing to keep the majority terrified from rebelling. Historically, this type of system always crumbled because as power and rule expanded, it was simply not sustainable—too many people, not enough enforcers.

Computers eliminate this sustainability "problem." Computers can control virtually every facet of commerce, communication and currency. Machines can relentlessly observe, trace and compute information about humans 24-7. They can shut down systems, deny access to information and resources, listen to phone calls and read texts.

The thinking machines are taking all manner of forms and functions. Drones, for instance, have become real game changers. They are the mobile eyes, ears and executioners of government. A little over 50 years after their practical implementation, these machines are just getting warmed up in terms of their constructive and lethal capacities.

The scary part is that we are basically still in the Neanderthal age of computing. Some futurists claim that Moore's Law, which describes exponential improvements in digital technology, indicates we'll have desktop computers with human levels of processing power within a couple of decades. Before the new century's midpoint, computers will be able to *improve themselves* at an incomprehensible rate. Science fiction? The smart phone in your pocket has more processing power than all the technology aboard the Apollo 13 mission.

But I digress. The only thing human beings crave more than money, sex and power is security...even if it means losing a certain amount of everything else. Shrewd leaders know that a good crisis should never be wasted. It's an opportunity to destroy or weaken enemies, thus securing even more power. As the world spins out of control, humans tend to give up more and more of their rights in hopes of gaining that ever elusive sense of safety and security.

Now, imagine the perfect global storm, the mother of all crises erupting that makes every other catastrophe in history look like a jaunt in the rain. Then, picture a governmental mindset seeking to leverage that crisis in a grab for absolute, total control...a government empowered with almost incomprehensible technological resources.

What could possibly stop something like this from happening? How would humanity ever stand a chance against such a powerful tyranny?

It would take someone with some amazing power, a lot of bravery and a conscience...

CHAPTER 1

A Flash in the Desert

Army Specialist Four Hiram Levy looked out of the window at the Nevada desert below as his plane approached the runway. Naively, he imagined this would be his last act of service. He was tired of military life and ready to be a civilian. And now, facing the uncertainty of yet another mission, the thought of returning to his parents' farm in Wisconsin gave him some comfort. His father was his hero. The former Marine had instilled in his heart the love for liberty and duty for country. As the plane's wheels skidded on the runway, Hiram wondered how a mission in Nevada would advance liberty. No one on board seemed to know any details; if they did, they weren't sharing. But Hiram could sense that this mission was going to be very different from any other he had ever been on during his tenure as a Ranger. His first clue had been the contents in his duffel bag—a solid white, head to toe, hazmat suit.

Running simultaneous with Hiram's wheels down, a classified briefing was to begin in the White House Situation Room in Washington,

D.C. The National Security Advisor, Henry Varick, was mentally reviewing his opening statement. He was confident, and for good reason. His significant influence over the President of the United States was growing with each crisis. Carefully, he had won the trust of the first Madam President. His self-assured voice created an illusion of stability, even in the face of bedlam. Henry Varick was the ultimate performer.

Varick opened the meeting with a series of extraordinary details on the terrorist "event," as he called it, in Nevada. A low-grade nuclear explosion had been confirmed, but it wasn't an attack so much as a proof of concept. The dirty bomb had been detonated simply as a showcase, proving their capabilities and willingness to execute. The chilling part of Varick's commencement was the terrorists' claim of possessing more devices—and they were ready to start real attacks with real damage very soon. They called themselves Threedom Fighters. Varick called them anarchists.

Henry Varick was nominated as the point person to handle communication with the Threedom Fighters. The scariest thing about the organization was how little intelligence sources seemed to know about them, making Varick the right person for the job. Years ago he penned a book sounding the alarm to new shadowy groups threatening the U.S. and the rest of the civilized world. He had accurately predicted this type of attack, making people's opinions malleable to his own in the wake of an offensive.

Varick was an ambitious public servant with an interesting twist. He was a self-proclaimed "patriotic globalist" who believed solutions to the increasing economic and military problems of the world would require aggressive global solutions, and the U.S. could lead the way. He was at the top of his class at Harvard Law School, with almost no realistic opposition to his debate skills. The influence he coveted was now in his hands. To the President, he was the number one counselor, and everyone in the cabinet knew it. Any ideas cabinet members had on security issues were channeled through him prior to reaching the President's desk.

Varick's path to power rested in his seemingly prophetic ability to project fear, uncertainty and doubt on matters of financial, energy and military threats. With no small touch of irony, he blazed a trail to power by accusing anyone who stood in his way as being intolerant. Unconventional means were justified when gigantic "national ends" were at stake, according to Varick. Terrorism in the name of religious extremism had paved the way for this line of thought. Enemy combatants were not entitled to the same protections of the law, even if they were citizens. Domestic suspects could be classified as extrajudicial prisoners if intelligence agencies could get Varick to pull the right strings, legally enabling "enhanced interrogation techniques" without the burden of the law's usual safeguards. Waterboarding and sensory deprivation still worked wonders in the art of information retrieval.

Those who raised questions regarding Varick's treatment of *any* terrorist suspects were marginalized. The man seemed at his best when righteously accusing media, civil liberty groups or congressional leaders of being soft on terrorism and national security, while condemning them for championing the rights of those who wanted to annihilate us. He never hesitated to position himself as the protector of liberty.

True to Varick's vision, a narrative had been birthed when somewhere in central Nevada on the morning of September 11, 2025, a flash of light outpaced a wave of sound careening across the desert floor. Someone had finally made good on the perpetually hyped "dirty bomb" threat. The following day, another device laid waste to a small portion of the Desert National Wildlife Range just west of Nevada's Hayford Peak. Now, no question remained about the threat to national security—the United States was under attack. No one, including the federal government, was offering any answers. Markets plummeted; the United States was gripped by panic. The terrorists had chosen seemingly innocuous sites north of Las Vegas, resulting in few casualties. Prevailing winds from the south directed the radiation away from populated areas, leading the public to conclude that these explosions were just a warning—the true threat was yet to be revealed.

A few tense hours after the detonation, the first-term U.S. President, Arlene Rutledge, appeared in a televised press conference. Unnerved by her cabinet meeting with Varick, she stowed her fear to assure a shaken public that the National Guard and Security Forces were being deployed to the scene to search for the perpetrators and to secure the perimeter. Promising the American people she would do everything in her power to protect them, she declared a state of martial law for Nevada (on Varick's recommendation), giving the U.S. Army a free hand to conduct reconnaissance missions throughout the entire state. In the interest of national security, certain areas would be off-limits to civilians and news agencies until further notice.

The next government official to address the nation was the Secretary of the Treasury, who declared that for five days the U.S. Stock Exchange and all national banks would be closed in an effort to regain a sense of calm. He was immediately followed by the Secretary of Defense with his guarantee that the U.S. Military was on high alert and that there would be "...no further detonations of Weapons of Mass Destruction on American soil," so long as he was in charge. Bloggers were the first to point out the curious omission of the standard phrase usually found in presidential addresses, "We shall not, under no circumstances, negotiate with terrorists." Perhaps decades of experience had led most Americans to believe that such a refusal was implied?

In the weeks following the initial explosions, as promised by the Secretary of Defense, no further terrorist attacks had ensued; yet a state of alert was maintained in Nevada. Anecdotal reports soon led to a rash of conspiracy theories...something was being kept under wraps, both from the general public and from the media.

Meanwhile, following the long, bumpy flight to the Nevada desert, Hiram trudged his way to Division Compound HQ—his new duty station for the next two years. After reporting to the commandant of the base, Hiram lugged his duffel bag over to the barracks where he found his quarters and his assigned bunk. Now late in the afternoon, he had just enough time to secure his bag and make it to the mess hall for supper. At sunset, all companies stood in formation as the base flag was lowered. Finally, it was time to fall out—back to the barracks for the night.

As Hiram was unpacking his duffel bag that evening he caught the attention of an Airborne Ranger standing nearby. His curiosity was piqued by Hiram's collection of artist's materials—pencils and paper, pen and ink, watercolors, etc. Hiram glanced at the sergeant, who despite his heavyweight boxer appearance seemed good-natured enough.

"Hey," he asked Hiram, "what's with all the sketchpads and charcoal pencils?"

Hiram sized up the man grinning at him. The name on his desert camouflage shirt above the right pocket read "Bin-Ali."

"Ain't nothing to sketch out here except sand, sky and the mythical 'terrorists,' if you can actually find one." They both laughed. The sergeant noted the military insignia on Hiram's left collar—M.I.— Military Intelligence.

"Oh," the sergeant remarked, "you M.I. guys draw pictures of the terrain...maps and all that, right?" Hiram nodded before assuming the lead in the conversation.

"I see your name is Bin-Ali."

"That's right—Sergeant First Class Abdul Bin-Ali."

"I'm Levy—Army Intel Specialist Four. Hiram Levy—sent here on special assignment. I don't see why a Muslim and a Jew can't work together." Laughing as he spoke, Bin-Ali quipped: "Man, I thought you were gonna say 'a black guy and a white guy.'" Hiram smiled in acknowledgement.

"You're right, I am Muslim—just like Muhammad Ali. I can fight like him too! I even speak a little Arabic. Picked it up at the Defense Language Institute in Monterey, California after I processed into the military from Compton, CA—my hometown. What's *your* story, Levy?"

"I'm from Wisconsin—lake country, and plenty of cows. My family's got a farm back there." Hiram was the next (and so far, last) in a long line of farmers who had lived for generations in a small Wisconsin town.

Their brief introduction was quickly punctuated by lights out. These unlikely comrades would have to wait until the morning to continue their friendly banter, which came easier than either had anticipated given their duties while out on maneuvers with Charlie Company. Over the next few weeks, the two would become inseparable.

When he wasn't philosophizing with Abdul, Hiram spent his time familiarizing himself with the colors of the landscape—the white sands, the foreboding mountains and the blue of the ceaseless sky. He wondered how long it would take until the desert landscape seemed more real to him than his memories of home in Wisconsin—the blues bluer and the whites whiter.

Hiram, Abdul and three others started running a daily reconnaissance mission for their company. Charlie Company consisted of
50 Airborne Rangers, including medics, officers and non-coms, as
well as transport vehicles—1 armored personnel carrier, 3 two-ton
trucks and 2 jeeps—and lots of ammo, small arms and grenade
launchers. Lunch, yet again, would consist of field rations. "Better
than Spam," Hiram mused.

Admittedly, Hiram's months of Army Intelligence training and his
excellent record in Airborne Jump School still left him unprepared
for what he ran into in Nevada.

Here he was in his own country fighting a war against terrorism. This
was a peculiar assignment. No air support meant no drones to fire
on the enemy position even if they located it. This was like a game,
but the rules were less clear than anything he'd experienced before.
Their mission was to search for terrorists, monitor radiation levels
and keep people away from the 30-mile perimeter from where
the explosions took place. Should the enemy be located, Charlie

Company was ordered not to fire unless fired upon. And every night, they came back to camp empty-handed.

During one particularly slow evening, Hiram was sitting on his bunk and had opened an old tattered leather Bible—which his father had given him as a boy. He began reading aloud to Abdul the ancient story of the Tower of Babel, found in the book of Genesis.

Following Hiram's recitation, Abdul, sitting on the bunk opposite Hiram's, put a question to his new friend: "This 'Tower of Babel'... that was somewhere near Baghdad, on the Euphrates, right?"

"As far as I know," responded Hiram.

"Yeah," said Abdul, leaning back as he stretched his arms and looked at the ceiling, "I've been there, and once was *enough!* But now I'm sitting here with you in Nevada with an unidentified enemy and we've got our hands tied—out of the frying pan, into the fire." The two men just shook their heads and laughed, trying to make the best of a bad situation.

"No, seriously," said Abdul, "do you mean to tell me that a long time ago everybody on this planet spoke the same language? I mean, what was it...? Was it like *Star Trek*, where *everybody* in the universe just happens to speak English? And I suppose all those great architects just crawled out of some cave, and decided to build the Mother of all Cities? And just *who* was runnin' the show?

"But that Tower of Babel must've been something to see. Fact is,

I've heard about another huge foundation for some new structure not far from here. Nobody seems to know what they are building. It could be another tower; the groundwork sounds as though it could shape up to be the largest thing anyone's ever seen."

Hiram strained to recapture Bin-Ali's attention.

"Don't forget the language issue. Throughout the world, the challenge to erect ever taller towers has never ceased, and throughout history there has always been an effort to unify language. In Western Europe, it was Latin—in the Mediterranean and in the Near East, it was Greek. For a time, Greek culture and language even influenced the Ancient Romans. For many years, French was the language of both statecraft and commerce. Now, in the computer age, everybody from India to Africa to Brazil wants to learn English. No wonder even the Klingons speak English." Abdul clenched his gut as he laughed at Hiram's callback.

Recovering his composure, he commented, "You know, Hiram, you might have something there, with this connection between world powers and the need for a global language.

"And now with the universal language of computers, ones and zeroes, information can be codified in just microseconds and transmitted anywhere on earth. You might say this *out-Nimrods* Nimrod. A single government with a monopoly on communication could literally rule the world."

* * *

The late night discussion with Abdul had stirred Hiram's imagination. His restless mind made it difficult for him to fall asleep. Then late in the night, as they often did, dreams came to him. While the majority of his visions were dismissed by his subconscious, tonight's left its mark. He was presented with an image of himself standing in the rough terrain of Nevada, alone, but not fearful. In the far distance, near Las Vegas, he saw what seemed like the Babylonian gate rising from the sand.

Hiram was jarred out of his vision by Abdul's good intentions. Shaking Hiram, Abdul announced, "Time to get up! You're talking crazy in your sleep!" A little embarrassed, Hiram wiped the sleep bug from his eyes and set his day in motion. With uncanny certainty, he knew the memory of this dream would persist.

* * *

Two years later, Hiram was honorably discharged from the Army. He had just arrived in Chicago, waiting for a connecting flight to Wisconsin. He was looking forward to seeing his parents, but he couldn't quit thinking about his tour in Nevada.

"What was the point of all that?" Hiram thought. Following his discharge, Hiram received a job offer from Soaring Eagle—a boys' home for high-risk teenagers near his parents' home. Meanwhile, Abdul returned to California to attend an engineering program.

"Home...," Hiram thought as he looked at his watch. "I can hardly wait." His flight was due to take off in less than an hour. To stave off that special kind of boredom an airport can force on a traveler, he removed his drawings from his duffel bag and laid them carefully on the floor next to him. There were several sketches that he had previously made of a "Virtual Tower." The conversation with Abdul had lingered, prompting an image he couldn't get out of his head, even after all this time.

A small child—a girl—came up to Hiram, attracted by his artwork. He was unaware that she was intently studying his work, but eventually her curiosity could not be subdued.

"Hello, mister, what's all this? What kind of a tower is *that*?" she asked, pointing. "Is it *real*?" Hiram was startled at first but quickly regained a friendly composure. He paused and smiled genuinely at her. "Well, darling," he said cryptically, "I don't know, it might be..."

CHAPTER 2

The Day the World Went Dark

It was a day like any other. The news outlets presented the usual litany of ills faced by a troubled world—emerging skirmishes, double-digit unemployment and destructive natural disasters at the hands of all the elements—doom and gloom.

However, at noon Eastern Standard Time, the world as everyone knew it ground to a startling halt. Without warning or visible cause, a pendulum of cataclysmic failure knocked out the first world's power grid. Only in the third world, where electricity was more of a luxury rather than a convenience, did the day-to-day routine continue nearly unabated.

In the blink of an eye, every light, every television, every automatic door and elevator—everything not powered by gas, wind or sun— simply stopped working. Microwave ovens, cash registers, coffee makers and air conditioners fell into a deep slumber. For eight hours, only idle speculation preserved man's sense of security and technical superiority. "This can't be worldwide, can it? Probably just a server failure like '03 or a lightning strike like Brazil in '99."

"I'm sure it's terrorists."

"It's gotta be an earthquake."

"Look what our elected officials screwed up this time."

The rumors flew as fast as uninformed mouths could spread them, but gossip entertains for only so long.

And then, just as quickly as the electrical power fell, it was resurrected. At precisely 8 p.m., a collective sigh of relief could be felt as people assumed they could return to their daily routines. Almost immediately, a text message lit up nearly every cell phone on the globe:

"VISIT CENTRALCOM.GOV FOR IMPORTANT INFORMATION REGARDING TODAY'S EVENTS."

Billions of fingers driven by curiosity, furor or even boredom, assaulted keyboards and touch screens. Their effort was rewarded with a simple graphic:

"Please stand by for a brief statement from the National Security Chairman regarding today's events at 8:15 p.m."

Patience had never been a prevalent global commodity, and now it was in even shorter supply. Modern world citizens, as a rule, didn't take kindly to electrical power outages. They expected quick and simple answers from their elected officials, not some vague message posted on a screen in the midst of such inconvenience. But the wait was a brief one, and as promised, the assured, gray-haired gentleman, Henry Varick, appeared precisely at 8:15 p.m. EST. He calmly began his speech to a worldwide audience...

"Good evening. Five years ago the United Nations implemented the Global Energy Network Consortium to better manage and more efficiently distribute the world's energy resources among each of the continent's consortiums." People remembered it well; the new energy system had in fact transformed energy into a new global monetary system, which transferred energy credits into actual currency. But now it was apparent the system had some serious weaknesses.

"Our systems were developed and maintained with state-of-the-art security safeguards thought to be nearly indestructible and impenetrable. Unfortunately, this system appears to have been internally compromised by traitors working with an international terrorist organization. By setting off a series of low-grade nuclear explosions coordinated with a devastating software attack, they have succeeded in shutting down significant portions of the world's power grid.

"Nonetheless, thanks to the brave men and women of the United Nations security force we have managed to regain temporary control of electrical power through several emergency-use substations.

As I stated earlier, these terrorists are highly trained members of a vast global network, but their success in sabotaging and compromising components of the global power grid is only temporary. Fortunately, emergency satellite up-links, broadcast facilities and Internet backbones remain under U.N. control operating off of emergency resources.

"Remain calm; be cautious. Worldwide panic is precisely what these terrorists wish to achieve through their actions. The attempts to hold hostage the United Nations *and* the 10 major nations on this planet have already failed. They have made their ransom demands clear to us: $10 billion in gold and the immediate release of their brothers in arms undergoing 'treatment' at Guantanamo Bay.

"I realize that many of you hearing my voice are waiting for the answers to the important questions: 'When will the power be restored permanently? Will our families be safe?' Honestly, we cannot tell you at this point. But I can assure you we stand with you and will *not* leave you in darkness. I must sign off now... This site and this message will continue to be available for those who can access it. Satellite phones, where available, may still provide you with intermittent contact if you have battery power, but the ground-based towers will likely run out of reserve power. I'm sorry— there's nothing more we can do at this time. We will update this site every 24 hours with further details as they become available. Remember—remain calm; be cautious and take the necessary steps to protect yourselves."

With that, power once again vanished. City skyscrapers stood like ghostly sentinels against the moonlit evening sky. The familiar comfort of the streetlights, faint blue glow of televisions and desktop computers, and even cell phone reception were but a fantasy. Darkness engulfed everything.

Mayhem accompanied the twilight as bands of looters took to the streets. From London to Athens, to Chicago to Beijing—all the major cities of the world became the center of rioting. The disaffected, disenfranchised portion of the population—long unemployed and without hope or privilege—saw opportunity in the fear and darkness to recoup that which life had not offered. A thieving rampage gradually spread from the cities to the outlying villages and suburbs. But wholesale robbery degenerated into rape and murder faster than anyone might have anticipated. As always, the innocent became the primary victims in a vicious syndrome of brutality. Police were overwhelmed by the spreading violence and many gave their lives defending people. Numerous traffic fatalities and city streets jammed with an outpouring of urban refugees were the result of non-existent traffic signals. Nobody slept that night, watching weary-eyed as the sun rose on a confused world.

For the remainder of day two of the energy disaster, all commerce remained at a standstill. Hospitals, thanks to their emergency back-up generators, were still up and running but were filled to capacity with the injured and the dying; the vast majority of patients were victims of break-ins and murder attempts. Many of the dead or injured lay undiscovered in neighborhood streets and even in their own homes.

As this day drew to a close, a needless text message was received yet again on cell phones worldwide—as if the world needed a reminder of the United Nations' promise to deliver information. All eyes were already turned toward centralcom.gov. As expected, at 8 p.m. sharp, 21st century conveniences sprung to life. The silver-tongued Henry Varick was back, this time broadcasting optimism to the globe. Updating his listeners on the latest details concerning the alleged worldwide search for the terror suspects, he assured a relieved audience that at that very moment U.N. forces in cooperation with Interpol were closing in on the key cells of this terrorist network.

And then, given the circumstances, Henry Varick's speech trailed off in an unexpected direction. He began to broadly describe the myriad of factors contributing to worldwide instability in the face of humanity's technological advances. By all accounts, as Varick saw it, the world as we knew it was headed for ruin. Crime, unemployment and environmental disasters were modern man's chief concerns. Buzzwords that have been tossed around by talking heads for decades made his list: fossil fuels, global warming, deforestation, soil erosion, overfishing and ocean acidification.

"A concerted effort," he stressed, "must be made to improve the global environment." This appeared to be the thrust of the second day's address. But again, with neither advance warning nor tact, this white-haired vestige of confidence and intrigue diverted attention to one specific topic—nuclear power.

"Foremost among these environmental hazards is the danger posed by nuclear accidents and the rogue use of dirty bombs." Referring specifically to Japan's Fukushima nuclear power disaster, the announcer pontificated for centralized control over nuclear plants worldwide.

Fukushima had released radioactive wastewater into the ocean, in turn, contaminating aquatic wildlife for miles offshore. By most estimates, decommissioning the reactor would take 40 years, with estimates on ocean water recovery as high as 300 years. Following Fukushima, new nuclear accidents occurred in N. Korea, China, Pakistan and the U.S., tipping the world's environment toward Armageddon. To prevent such accidents from ever occurring in the future, joint government protocols had been established to ensure energy safety standards in every nation worldwide.

"Certainly," said Varick in a comforting tone, "no one could argue with such a reasonable action. This matter was too important to ignore—both for the safety of our children and for the welfare of our planet."

The spokesman concluded his 10-minute broadcast with an inexplicable special announcement:

"Unfortunately, electrical power will again be shut down immediately following this broadcast. We have no choice, given the severity of the damage in key areas." Collective ire rose from a global audience anxious for a return to normal life.

"Tomorrow evening I will be joined by a number of world leaders. By that time, we believe the U.N. and major world powers will have the crisis well in hand." Abruptly, centralcom.gov switched to a static U.N. logo.

Everyone knew that the second night of this primitive atmosphere would bring further wanton brutality. Battle lines had already been drawn while the sun was still up, and in the absence of any real police protection, vigilantes formed defense committees. They had taken the necessary steps to protect their property, their homes and their lives. After the previous night's violence, no quarter would be given. Neighborhoods banded together to keep inner-city violence from spreading further into the suburbs. The world's citizens would face at least one more night of unrest with overcast skies blanketing the streets in absolute darkness.

Neighbors, who previously struggled to remember each other's names, formed vital alliances and banded together to protect one another's homes. Anyone in possession of a firearm had plenty of company that night. Even normally peaceful citizens were now armed with whatever weapons they could lay their hands on—knives, axes, pool cues—and the desperate even wielded chainsaws. These people refused to become victims of senseless violence—they would fight. Spontaneously, neighbors became close friends and family. Tonight, there would be no more rapes, theft or murder—not if *they* could help it.

That night, violent gangs again tried to overtake the suburbs, but this time they were met with semi-automatic weapons, handguns, shotguns, guard dogs, hunters and former military personnel. Time and again, attacks were successfully abated. The mobs were vastly overmatched and outgunned. The following day and on into the evening, neighborhood defense forces kept a vigilant eye out for trouble. Even cops finally joined in, admitting that under the circumstances vigilante action was acceptable.

On night three of the outage, everyone was once again sitting in front of a screen, waiting for someone to do something. Every household remained vigilant; husbands and wives peered out of windows on high alert. Punctually, at 8 p.m., electricity surged through the global stage for a nervous and weary audience.

"Good evening, citizens of the world, young and old! We are aware of the hardships many of you have had to endure during this regrettable breakdown of authority. Many of you are frightened, tired and hungry. But tonight I bring you hope! Most of you will recognize the faces of those joining me as your elected leaders."

The studio camera pulled back to bring into frame the entire group of heads of state, from presidents to prime ministers, seated about a semi-circular conference table. They all faced the audience, with the announcer seated in the center. Henry Varick, with his usual air of confidence, continued his speech...

"And now, we are pleased to announce that the crisis appears to be over. The terrorist threat has been subdued, and tonight at midnight, Eastern Standard Time, power throughout the world will once again be restored on a *permanent* basis. Please take any precautions you deem necessary in the meantime to protect yourselves, your property and your families.

"Finally, an historic announcement! To provide for the safety of our planet and to guarantee the prevention of future terrorist attacks, it is with great honor that we declare a global partnership representing a new international union that will improve and integrate individual sovereign authority as well as the continental energy consortiums. Our union of nations has been established for the benefit of every man, woman and child around the world.

"This is also an international Bill of Rights for everyone—a world government coalition that shall be known as the Universal Order. The U.N., the World Court and the 10 major industrialized nations of the world have all expressed their support. The representatives seated here with me will appear in a televised press conference tomorrow morning. Each nation will also be addressed by its respective head of state, who will provide a detailed briefing on a protective and painstakingly crafted International Security Plan. We believe this international partnership will help prevent this kind of attack from ever happening again. In the days ahead, as energy distribution stabilizes, you will learn the details of how much danger every man, woman and child was in during the last two days. Thank you all for your courage and support in the midst of this unprecedented worldwide crisis."

Centralcom.gov now signed off with the newly designed crest of the Universal Order. In everyone's home the flashlights came back on, and rifles reappeared from inside the windows. For now, it was business as usual.

CHAPTER 3

The Universal Order Protocol

As promised, precisely at midnight, power throughout the world was restored. The afterglow of this "achievement" would defuse a last-minute change in the following morning's proceedings.

It was Saturday morning, a pleasant day in April. Abruptly, Universal Order officials had relegated President Arlene Rutledge's press conference to a simple briefing—*no* questions from the press. This live broadcast was set for 11 a.m. Eastern Standard Time. In light of the recent wave of violence, all the necessary security precautions had been taken. On schedule and without exception, major over-the-air and cable networks and centralcom.gov began their broadcast of the President's speech to the nation. Simultaneously, nations around the world were addressed by their respective heads of state.

To the bewilderment of a global audience, not a single world leader had much to say about the power outage. Yes, it had been a severe interruption, but one that had met with a rapid resolution. And yes, the culprits had been detained. Instead of elaborating on the details, the heads of state chose to focus on something they saw as an even greater threat to the world's inhabitants. The President paused, taking a single deep breath before launching into the real gist of her speech.

"What I am about to say may shock many of you, but we have another crisis that must be addressed at this time or we will face even more serious consequences than we just experienced. The recent dramatic fluctuation in world currencies has left our economies wide open to manipulation. These currencies are frequently subject to artificial devaluation, often playing into the hands of unscrupulous individuals who scam the inefficiencies and volatility of the currency market.

"The U.S. currency is the world's reserve currency, which has for decades added to the stability of financial markets around the world. But in recent years China has challenged our reserve status and has offered the world a gold-backed yuan as an alternative reserve currency. This has brought a considerable disruption to the financial markets, and consequently the U.S. dollar has taken a hit as money circulated overseas has flooded back in to the U.S. as other countries opt for the yuan as the currency of choice. It is in the interest of both our nations to stabilize this situation. The devaluation of

the U.S. dollar has had a severe impact on their holding of U.S. treasuries. We have come to an agreement—a compromise—for the good of the world.

"In consultation with both the Secretary of the Treasury and Congress, I have determined that in order to protect our national interests we must embrace drastic action. With the unanimous approval of Congress, the United States has reached an agreement with China and joined with other major nations in signing the Universal Order Protocol. The primary tenet of this Protocol is the establishment of a new global digital currency. Further details will follow from the Secretary of the Treasury and the Chairman of the Federal Reserve. To guarantee the solvency of this new currency, the U.O. will secure and consolidate all gold and silver deposits currently held in national reserves. Ongoing revenue to support the Universal Treasury will be generated by taxes levied on all international commerce. There will be no 'tax havens' or 'financial hideouts' for those unwilling to pay their fair share for a safer and more transparent world.

"*All* financial institutions, because of corruption at all levels and their collusion both in money-laundering schemes and currency manipulation, are to be administered by a consortium—one comprised of the 10 major world powers, including the United States—the U-10.

"To achieve this in the most efficient manner, each nation is requesting that its citizens participate in the 'Bring the Wealth Home' program should they happen to have funds overseas. People need to entrust their resources to their respective nation— their domicile. This must be done within the next 120 days; if you miss the deadline you will be unable to make the necessary currency exchange. We ask this in light of the recent tragedy, and in order to safeguard the lives and livelihoods of every man, woman and child on the planet."

Noting the severity of each statement, one cascading after the other, the press could no longer contain their curiosity. "Madam President...!" Immediately, the Secret Service moved to intervene.

"I'm sorry," the President responded in her defense, "this is a briefing, *not* a press conference. Please save your questions for White House Spokesman Mr. Adkins. Now if I might continue...

"A second aspect of this Protocol deals with the matter of international energy security; a recent security breach led to a crisis which is undoubtedly still on everyone's mind. I am truly sorry for those of you who have suffered hardship throughout the crisis. Thankfully, that is now *behind* us. What we have *before* us is a challenge. By supporting the U.O. initiative and working together with our international partners in peace, we can mount an international defense against domestic and global terrorism. By creating a worldwide database, the U.O. will be able to thwart any future attacks like the most recent one that held the world hostage for three days. Sharing information is paramount—we must learn to trust the collectors of confidential information. Terrorist cells capable of premeditated attacks might be hiding anywhere; timely information can expose them.

"A third proviso of this U.O. Protocol, which I have signed into law, is predicated on a leap in nanotechnology. Think of buying on credit—a wonderful idea for its time, but one that has led to immeasurable hardship: credit card theft, identity theft and breaches of security at banks and retail outlets everywhere. Electronic theft and fraud on a global scale has become so prevalent that it threatens families everywhere. Your or your children's financial past, present and future could be excised without warning.

"Our new digital currency will be as good as gold and even more secure. What if some cashier could simply scan a tag implanted in your wrist, one located just above the back of your hand? It could neither be stolen nor copied. All recorded purchases would be logged into a central database for your convenience. Your discounted invoice would be sent to your home address at the end of each month. Of course, this program would be a voluntary one. Let me stress, for anyone who chooses it, that cash is still an option—but you forfeit the discount. The discount is offered only as an efficiency incentive, payable to the customer for simplifying millions of transactions worldwide. Centralization and cooperation are what the U.O. hopes to achieve through this program, and it's our responsibility to be tolerant and open-minded toward change, willing to accept progress in order to protect our children and our way of life.

"Now, I would like to draw your attention to one further proviso of the Universal Order Protocol. I have just spoken of tolerance; please bear this in mind when I tell you it's time to convene a worldwide convocation of the major religious organizations—the Roman Catholic Church, Protestant denominations, leaders of Judaism, Imams of the Muslim faith and various representatives of other Eastern religions. All of them are to be convened in Jerusalem in an effort to establish a new understanding of religious tolerance. The world has seen enough religious strife and violence: Muslims against Hindus, Hindus against Christians, Christians against Muslims and even Catholics who continue to fight with Protestants. *Enough!* We must have peace and tolerance at all costs."

The small, live audience began an unenthusiastic but politically correct applause.

"The constant conflicts between Israel and the Arab countries must cease. The U.O. leadership will enter into serious negotiations starting with Israel, Palestine, Iran, Syria and Egypt to bring about the immediate cessation of conflict, in order to establish permanent peace in our time. The Middle East cannot, and will not, drain the resources of the United Nations and now the Universal Order. Peace will be enforced by the World Court, and the Universal Order will be its advocate. Once again, Isaac and Ishmael will walk hand in hand as brothers for the higher calling of their father Abraham.

"I cannot yet be specific as to the proposed agenda for this conference. The Universal Order will see to the arrangements and is mandating attendance. On this note, I wish to conclude my address. Thank you for your patience and perseverance during these difficult times."

With these words the President strode away from the podium, with Secret Service agents fending off the swarm of agitated White House press correspondents.

CHAPTER 4

Hiram—Called to Action

Hiram was ruminating again, this time in the peaceful confines of the rustic cabin he'd constructed on his parents' farm. Civilian life had not quite been the harmonious experience he had expected. The world had turned upside down and he found himself caught in conflict with Universal Order's accession of safety. He gazed into the fireplace with Charlie, his big and fluffy Tabby cat resting comfortably on his lap. The fire had burned low, but added a welcome incandescence to the dark room. Hiram often got so wrapped up in his thoughts that he didn't bother to turn on any lights as dusk approached. A couple of emergency candles danced on the table, seemingly in rhythm with Hiram's thoughts. Occasionally, he glimpsed the snowflakes floating in front of the picture window he loved so much. Aside from the moonlight reflected on the snow-covered ground, there was no artificial light around this place. Hiram liked it that way. You could really see the stars here. Resting in his lap, Charlie purred softly, completely satisfied with the entire arrangement.

Hiram's memories drifted to his former brothers-in-arms. The trouble with war was that it played on your mind, particularly the area of suffering. Hiram had seen a lot of it. But it wasn't just the suffering that bothered him; it was the sheer madness and impenetrable mystique of his tour in Nevada. Nothing had ever come of it—no enemy combatants, no dirty bombs and no answers.

"What the hell were we fighting for?"

Although he struggled to process it all, Hiram's faith did not waiver. He maintained the quiet hope that someday he would comprehend the meaning of that heartbreaking bugle call as it had echoed across so many empty wastelands where his friends had made the ultimate sacrifice.

But something else was gnawing at him now, and he became increasingly unsettled. Charlie detected this agitated change in his master's mood and distanced himself from it, sauntering off to a more comfortable location. Initially distracted by the sudden departure of his feline companion, Hiram tried to relax and allow his mind to drift. But every time, his thoughts found their way back to some disturbing ideas.

He had been in many firefights and seen a lot of vicious situations— terrorists, insurgents, rebels and paramilitary factions—but never the unnerving desolation he felt in Nevada.

No encounters? No evidence of enemy camps? And the detonation site had been too perfect. Such a remote location was not a place anyone could find without superior satellite assistance. And then it would take some sophisticated equipment to simply move men and materials into that location. Also, detonating any kind of nuclear device is not a simple process. He had been in more than one internment camp. None of the insurgents he had ever helped interrogate could handle detonating such sophisticated ordinance. But he didn't meet everybody, and of course all that could be explained away with coincidence and "first ever" explanations...

What bothered him most was the complete lack of intel. It was no secret that the NSA tracked billions of calls daily, keeping dossiers on anybody and everybody who could be considered a problem (and even those who weren't). Air fleets of drones tracked every foot of our borders and robotic scanners were at every entry point, not to mention the battalion of old-fashioned canine. For over 40 years we've had satellites that could read a newspaper from 30,000 feet. It was too clean for any group of terrorists. This was top drawer, weapons-grade precision only a nation could muster. His whole mission had been a fool's errand.

When all other options were eliminated, he was left only with the hypothesis that a group of wealthy, powerful opportunists connected to disillusioned military leaders had precipitated the whole thing to create a world economic crisis. But that would be the greatest power grab since the Roman Empire.

But what really scared him was the down side... The disasters called for martial law that didn't go away. But they didn't call it martial law—they called it a "protocol." The protocols were set up to keep the peace, to keep people safe. From the outside, the Order's recursive decrees were almost humorous; in essence, they were not going to tolerate intolerance anymore. After all, that was the root of all our problems... But nobody was on the outside. Sensitive topics carried language safeguards now, particularly in areas of discussion that had anything to do with religion, sexuality or absolutes.

All "truth" had to bow to the facts regardless of what you believed or what your values system held to be true. And the government determined all the "facts." Tolerance protocols demanded the greatest good for the greatest number—unadulterated utilitarianism. Open public discussion had incited so much violence and governmental strife that Congress had appropriated all communication entities in a move to protect national interests and citizen safety.

It had all started early in the decade when presidents, Congress and even the judicial branch began controlling their images at obsessive levels. Press pools became dinosaurs of the past. The government actually provided news outlets with all the new material, and that included their own footage, photos and staged interviews. It was clean, tidy, best-foot-forward stuff meant to strangle the press into compliance—a brutal winnowing process. Those who produced positive stories got more access. Those who questioned and distributed negative stories got marginalized and eventually had their credentials removed. In the most extreme cases, they were arrested for breaking the protocols.

Hiram could not process the ramifications of it all. "Was this present state of affairs inevitable? How much of our freedom have we traded for 'stability'?"

Hiram's concentration was suddenly broken by the wail of an emergency siren penetrating the cracked window. Springing from his rocking chair, he looked out into the starlit night for any signs of smoke against the horizon. It may have been an ambulance siren, or that of a patrol car, but as a volunteer firefighter he had instinctively gotten to his feet. Within seconds the dispatcher's voice on his one-way radio repeatedly read out an address. Familiar with the area in question, Hiram quickly exchanged his slippers for boots and made a dash for the door.

When he arrived at the scene he surveyed a large, old four-story house that had been converted to a low-cost tenement. Now it was engulfed in flames rising into the night sky; smoke was billowing out of the windows of the lower three floors. Hiram's attention was drawn to a woman frantically trying to break through the police cordon surrounding the building. "My daughter..." she screamed waving her arms, "she's still in there.... My God, someone do something!" Hiram ran up to her, flashing his fireman's badge at the patrolmen. Hiram's eyes shone bright with focus and intensity; looking the woman full in the face and grabbing her by the shoulders, he asked one question: "Where?" The woman collected herself and pointed, "The apartment right next to the staircase on the third floor.... Her name is Jenny... Jenny."

Hiram ran for the building's door, which had already been demol-
ished by the other firemen. As he charged through the shattered
entrance, without breaking pace, he threw on a coat and helmet
tossed to him by a crewman.

"Hiram, you forgot your oxygen mask," the firefighter yelled.

The girl's mother stood by helplessly as the police officers tried to
keep her calm. Overcome, she fell to her knees. She prayed for the
safety of Jenny and her newfound only hope.

Kneeling there, staring into the raging flames, it seemed as if an
eternity went by. Precipitated only by the sound of cracking wood
and dispersed embers, Hiram burst out of the building with Jenny
securely in his arms. His friend Joe immediately ran to his assistance. "Damn it," he exclaimed, "you're on fire, Levy!" Hiram fell
to the ground; he handed off the bundle he had been carrying. As
Joe scanned the child for injury, another firefighter rushed to wrap
Hiram in a fireman's coat, smothering the flames. Immediately,

Jenny's mother was there to take her child in her arms. All three were rushed to a nearby ambulance for inspection.

Hiram's courage that day proved to be an inspiration to many in the town; he had become a local hero. Following a few days of rest in the cabin, he returned to the Boys' Ranch where he now worked as a counselor. He was, of course, greeted by several boys playfully accosting him. "Hey," they laughed, "you crazy!?! Running into a fire like that?" Hiram was familiar with their tone—he knew that this was just another form of expressing respect. He thought more of their respect for him than he did the publicity surrounding his recent act of heroism. This was *his* family.

Unfortunately, there were some in the community who were not impressed by Hiram's bravery. These were the men who held the reins of power, the enforcers of the Protocols. Hiram had already crossed swords with these men in town hall orientation meetings, demonstrating the courage to resist the "tolerance laws." *He had publicly refused to agree to the general directives promoted by the Universal Order's Protocol.*

His intolerance had been well noted by the local U.O. officials. Hiram was not only a hero, he was an outspoken opponent of the U.O. "relativist" position on absolute truth. He had the audacity to question some of "the facts."

CHAPTER 5

An Intolerable Resurrection

Soaring Eagle put Hiram in a unique position on the front lines of one of America's toughest social problems—fatherless boys. Hiram had been blessed with a father who cared for and loved him. He had always known he had a good dad, but it wasn't until he served in the military that he felt the burden of boys who were not so fortuitous. The army was full of men with no direction, purpose or goals. Military service was their last chance.

Most of the boys were at the ranch as a result of brushes with the law. Many had been abused in various, often violent, ways. As a result, discipline problems flowed in a steady stream, one after another. So, one of the first things Hiram had established upon his arrival was a reward system. Carrots were better than sticks, he knew from experience. For many of the boys, this was their first encounter with the idea that responsibility could bring reward. And Hiram knew that by giving them honest responsibilities he could empower them to a better future.

As a reward for incident-free behavior over the past month, Hiram took four boys from Soaring Eagle to an outdoor concert on a spectacular spring day. They made quite a foursome—these guys were almost his size, and he was a towering specimen! Hiram made no effort to hide his laughter as he watched them arrange themselves in his crew cab like Tetris pieces while he sat comfortably in the driver's seat.

Windows down, the drive was pleasant but fairly uneventful. Typical of male bonding experiences, they volleyed insults for most of the trip. Hiram was thankful the venue wasn't too far. As they inched toward the gigantic sloped meadow, which formed a natural amphitheater, music began to pour in to the truck's open windows.

Following a frisking and unceremonious validation of their tickets, Hiram and his entourage ambled through the crowd searching for a good view. The sight of kids dancing, singing and generally having the time of their lives was inspiring and breathtaking to these newcomers. The environment wasn't what Hiram would have chosen—beer was the unofficial beverage of choice and pot smoke held steady in the air thanks to the thousands of revelers blocking the wind. There was a distinct lack of clothing given the temperature. It all reminded him that youth could rarely be swayed from making bad decisions. On second thought, how the hell did he get talked into making this the "reward"? But keeping his guys within arm's reach, he managed to keep a smile throughout the evening; he could tell the boys appreciated every second.

The venue had a unique mix of stages. It was a smorgasbord of musical styles. If you got tired of one band, you could brave the journey to another stage. As a result, the crowds were in a constant state of restless motion. After three hours of wishing he had brought earplugs, Hiram signaled it was time to go home. Early in the day the boys realized they weren't going to meet any girls, so they didn't bother to argue.

As Hiram's entourage was making their way out of the park, snaking through a gradually thinning crowd, the scraping sound of structural failure pierced the air. All five wheeled around in time to see a piece of scaffolding fall from the stage directly into the crowd below. As a segment of the crowd rushed to the base of the stage, Hiram elbowed his way back through the mob, boys in tow. An eternity of maneuvering through the chaos finally gave birth to a tumultuous scene. Trapped beneath a tangle of cables and steel scaffolding lay a beautiful young Asian woman—a victim of timing and circumstance.

Hiram quickly assessed the situation as he dialed 911. No sooner was the call made than he began clicking out orders to the guys to gather pieces of scaffolding, support pipes and any heavy wooden boards. Rigging several pieces together into a makeshift leverage system, and with the muscle of his young friends, he was able to carefully free her from entanglements within a matter of minutes.

She was certainly unconscious, and bleeding from the nose and ears. Hiram concluded at the very least she had suffered a concussion and was in shock. But more importantly, he realized *she wasn't breathing.* "She's dead!" screamed a frantic companion, losing the battle of composure over her friend's inanimate body. Hiram grabbed her wrist and pressed his ear against the left side of her chest—searching, listening for a pulse...none. Without delay he started CPR, gently lifting her head so he could breathe into her mouth while intermittently applying repeated pressure to her chest—a futile attempt. Behind him, the hysterics grew.

"She's dead! Oh my God!"

Out of options, still kneeling and holding the girl's lifeless body, Hiram closed his eyes, pulled her a little closer in his arms and lifted his face toward the heavens as if to offer a prayer. He uttered just one request: "Live!" No one seemed to grasp his intention. What could he possibly hope to achieve by merely speaking a word? Surely, this one was lost to eternity. But something happened that no one had ever experienced—the distinct arrival of a presence.

A presence so powerful no one could describe it without sounding like some kind of fanatic. No one would ever admit that. No one heard anything or saw anything, but everyone felt it. Immediately after the feeling dissipated, a sign of life appeared. The small throng of concertgoers in the immediate vicinity gasped in unison as they saw one of her fingers move—then, her chest rose and fell ever so slightly. She let out a soft, labored moan. The crowd stepped back, uncertain and a bit fearful of what might happen next. They had encountered something that was wonderful and terrifying all at the same time.

In the distance, a siren finally cut through the tension—the ambulance was on its way. Her friends broke down and dropped to the girl's side. "Mei-ling, you're alive!" Confused, but recognizing her name, the injured girl turned her head slightly, cracked open her lovely, almond-shaped eyes and tried to say something. Hiram caringly motioned for her to rest, promising her he would stay by her side until paramedics arrived. The crowd began cheering and clapping.

By the time paramedics finally cleared a path to Mei-ling, talk of a miracle was already circulating. Fearing the attention this would generate, Hiram thought it wise to make a speedy exit before an even brighter spotlight shone on him and his entourage. However, their exodus was far from subtle. Several people followed him, continuing to clap their hands; others cheered unabashedly. All five found it a little disconcerting. But the heroes did not linger.

Many had doubts about what they had just seen with their very own eyes. Skeptics refused to believe they had witnessed an actual miracle. But those who *did* believe told friends, family and acquaintances what they had personally witnessed.

CHAPTER 6

Attraction

The whole incident had succeeded in stirring up a narrative of hope, confusion and fear all at the same time; Hiram knew everything that had happened would stir great controversy...even though a greater good had overcome a horrific tragedy. Upon hearing the calls for assistance over the police band, the local news media immediately redirected a few mobile news crews to the venue to report on the accident. Accordingly, several concertgoers would later appear on the evening news with their wild stories. While some claimed they had witnessed a miracle—that a man had raised a girl from the dead—others flat out denied it. The fact that some of the interviewees were obviously somewhat inebriated did not lend credence to the scene. Many were cut short as it became obvious they only wanted a chance to slovenly swear on TV or screech "Hi!" to their mom and sorority. Nonetheless, controversy grew, garnering more attention day by day.

These were precisely the kind of incidents that the Universal Order feared. The idea that any kind of unexplainable incident would encourage young people to engage in open discussions about the existence of miracles was more than merely ludicrous—it was dangerous. Miracles implied a higher authority than the Universal Order. And these leaders *could not tolerate* any challenge to their authority. Their rational beliefs were not to be questioned by some random metaphysical quirk! The very idea of it was an insult to their intelligence and to their ultimate authority.

Science had learned to extend life, but had yet to solve the problem of death. Such concerns transformed to obsessions for the higher-ups at the Universal Order. They wanted to live forever and assumed everyone else felt the same. Although this lay outside their power, a temporary solution to a permanent problem was surmised—suspended biological existence for the elderly and the handicapped. Modern medicine had managed to prolong life, but the attendant costs were staggering.

As a result, the world's treasury had gone bankrupt. An immediate win/win was necessary to return solvency. After careful consideration, the U.O. officials made it policy to target social sectors of paucity unable to generate significant tax revenue. It was a tough compromise, but the new generation was well armed to make such life and death decisions.

The primary tenet of their blueprint was limiting access to healthcare without causing mass panic. Their solution: At the age of 85, unless exempt, individuals would be indefinitely cryogenically frozen. If the U.O. were to be believed, suspension was not syn-onymous with death. It was merely a "temporary hibernation of the life processes offset by the promise of revival." Unsurprisingly, not everyone bought in.

Any talk of resurrection merely served to undermine the credibility of the Order's cryogenics program—it would subtract from the public's confidence in this new utopia. The fact that he had seem-ingly resurrected a human being made Hiram Levy the focus of a lot of attention...both good and bad. Because of his newly minted reputation as a miracle worker, Hiram was now a target. Many in the U.O. would not see his heroic act as any kind of humanitarian effort; they would see it as a question-generating threat to all their authority. Animus building, it was quite unlikely that the Universal Order would ignore or forget about him.

Weeks after the incident, Hiram received a call from a Captain Shih. He quietly and humbly introduced himself as the father of Mei-ling, none other than the young woman who Hiram had rescued. He invited Hiram to dinner so the family could thank him personally for rescuing their only child. A meeting was arranged for the following week at one of the finest restaurants in the nearby city.

Upon meeting the family around an elegantly decorated dinner table, Hiram was immediately struck by the unusual pairing of Captain Shih's Asian ancestry and his wife's Mediterranean descent. Hiram's eyes drifted to Mei-ling. In the midst of the accident, covered in sweat, dust and dirt, he had failed to notice that she was ravishing. He was completely taken by her spectacular countenance—she seemed designed from everything that defined beauty. This was the kind of woman who made strong men weak. Some light conversation with wine to match loosened the grip of what was initially a cumbersome meal, and inevitably the ice melted.

But besides Mei-ling's beauty and sweet intelligence, Hiram discovered he had much in common with Shih, and it wasn't all of a military nature. The problem was that Hiram found Mei-ling's beauty disconcerting. Obviously distracted, Hiram struggled with the content of Shih's words. Slowly, it dawned on him that the two shared similar concerns regarding the loss of personal liberty in the United States and the rest of the world, not to mention the overarching tone of authoritarian mindset in governmental communications.

The topics were all of such interest that Hiram and Captain Shih agreed to meet again in a place less public. Simultaneously love-struck and keenly interested in Shih's views, Hiram also noticed that Mei-ling was showing a keen interest in their topic of conversation. As the evening wore down, he found himself a bit anxious that he might not ever see this incredible woman again. So he carefully waited until Mei-ling offered a particularly good insight on a governmental mandate and then casually asked Mei-ling if she might join them in the next meeting. She smiled and coyly said she would have to check her schedule. Hiram saw the game immediately, given that her smart watch was clearly visible. Now he had hope...

During goodbyes, Hiram intentionally positioned himself so that

Mei-ling would be the last one he addressed among the farewells. He gallantly tried to conceal his obvious attraction for Mei-ling as he politely reached out to shake her hand. As their hands touched, she gently and quickly slid both her arms around his upper torso and pulled him close for a soft kiss on the cheek. She held him tightly and moved her lips toward his right ear and whispered, "Thank you!" As she spoke, her lips gently brushed his earlobe. Hiram's pulse quickened to a level he hadn't felt since his last firefight. His eyes dropped for a moment, but he quickly regained his composure and looked straight into her glowing, light brown eyes. "So, maybe we'll meet again, huh?"

Hiram kicked himself all the way home. When it came to love, this hero was a bit shy. And that's what Mei-ling liked about him...

CHAPTER 7

An Intolerant Man

The Universal Order's lust for control knew no bounds. It sought to extend its grip over every social institution known to man. It wasn't satisfied with controlling just government, media, business and academia—it wanted to control even the family and the church. Government learned long ago that non-profit organizations were easily manipulated and controlled by threatening their tax-exempt status. The loss of financial benefits guaranteed their destruction. Churches under the Universal Order's rule had to make dramatic changes in what they said and taught in order to survive, or they were forced to go underground. Nothing could be communicated that would cause any imagined or perceived insult to any other group of people. As a result, many churches simply disappeared from public view and a host of new ones rose up.

Hiram decided to visit one of the newer, U.O. approved churches—a sanctuary that met the standards for tolerance. He'd heard that such places made significant contributions to the Order's coffers.

As a man of faith, he wanted to see if this one offered more than commentary on everyday life. Taking a seat in the back, he didn't presume this sanctioned chapel would be a false church. He hadn't come looking for trouble; he had come to worship his God.

The building had more of a theatrical, commercial atmosphere rather than a liturgical design. It felt like a mall with a stage. The Universal Order had determined that churches appealed to large segments of the affluent, upper middle class that liked its comfort. And they needed to contribute to the greater good of society. So everything from coffee shops, bookstores, restaurants and "religious items" were encouraged in this house of worship. The goods were sold at "above normal" prices to accommodate the special religious tax that was levied on all legitimately sanctioned, faith-based organizations. The service was broken into segments that paused about every 15 minutes to promote one of the businesses in the facility. There were even animals involved! It was, of course, the humanitarian outreach mission auctioning off homeless animals every week for the largest donation. Everything from birds to snakes to kittens played on stage. The highest bidders threw their money into large "baskets of mercy" on the stage. People could feel good knowing they did something positive for a helpless creature. Those who led "the worship" were more like auctioneers or carnival barkers than pastors.

Hiram, uncharacteristically, was unable to contain his anger in the face of such hypocrisy. He knew that these "showmen" were mocking everything he believed in. As the assistants marched to the stage to transport the mercy baskets laden with cash, Hiram could take it no longer. Moving to intercept, he reached deep into his memory to pull out a running block move from his high school football days. Each of his blocks sent a basket of mercy donation vouchers fluttering across the stage. When every basket had been overturned, Hiram sent the tables of merchandise flying, chasing after the early purchase vouchers.

If any confusion remained as to his opinion of the U.O.'s interpretation of "liturgical commerce," Hiram clarified his stance by snatching the microphone from the hand of one terrified stage assistant, proclaiming, "You're giving organized crime and whorehouses a bad name!" To his surprise, a group of parishioners took issue with his statement and attempted to wrangle the mic from his hands. But Hiram, a skilled wrestler of generous size and stature, broke free and used the state of confusion to escape through a side door before the angry crowd could catch him. Although lost in his own temper, he still felt empathy toward the people who were being taken in so easily by these snake oil salesmen.

As reports of Hiram's behavior at the church reached the local U.O. safety office, swift action was set in motion. The following day, Soaring Eagle was overrun by the authorities. The boys tried to protect Hiram by misdirecting or refusing to cooperate, but Hiram soon realized that their efforts were creating more problems than they were solving and he surrendered without incident. During the short escort to a U.O. van, he kept his silence and an empty, downward gaze.

Hiram's arrest had been inevitable—he had already aroused the suspicion of the U.O. authorities. The Universal Order had established protectorates in cities and towns across America. Within the walls of the U.O. Protectorate, stasi-esque machinations reigned supreme. Remnants of U.S. authority had no power here. Hiram was quickly ushered by van to the Chicago Protectorate. There were no lawyers to call, no lawsuits—he was simply at their mercy. Torture was not officially tolerated, but many suspected that the U.O. officials would resort to enhanced interrogation techniques to fulfill their agenda. Upon his arrival, Hiram would neither answer their questions nor sign their affidavits, holding his tongue under mental and emotional anguish.

The accusation was "intolerance," now considered a hate crime under U.O. rule. To coerce a confession, enhanced interrogation techniques indeed preceded his trial. The U.O. agents were experts in psychological torture, yielding accurate results but leaving no marks and falling just short of Geneva guidelines for inhumane treatment. As he suffered, he accepted that no satisfaction derived from some previous good deed could lessen his agony. His mind, wracked with fear and loathing, begged his spirit to yield—to break rather than resist. Hiram Levy's conscious mind lay shattered. Yet his bravery denied him the choice of giving in to the pain and humiliation. Standing before his captors, he held his peace and proffered no confession.

The inquisitors stared down Hiram and bellowed: "What insolence! You are nothing but an intolerant traitor. Our new society must be protected from radical fanatics such as you! We are watching!"

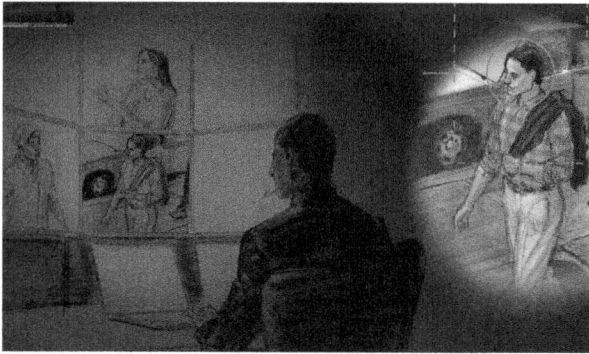

In response, Hiram quietly asked, "Who's protecting me?" Infuriated by this simple question, the inquisitor pointed to a computer monitor sitting on a desktop nearby. "There is all the truth we need, period. This monitor is connected to the heart of the M-5 computer—we call it 'the BEAST'—the largest, most powerful computer the world has ever known. It is both your judge *and* jury. It knows everything about you, Mr. Levy. The BEAST contains volumes of data procured by our surveillance teams. We have a record of every word you have uttered over the past several years. The computer has known about 'the man Hiram' for some time now. Our evidence against you is overwhelming, and the BEAST has never lost a case yet."

Hiram did not bow or cower, but said nothing. And for his "insolence" he was dragged back to his prison cell and dropped onto a frigid stone floor where he lay alone and incredibly cold. Hiram no longer had even the strength to lift himself into the crude cot that reeked of unanswered prayers and destitute hope. Lying face down on the floor and in a state of delirium, his mind soothed his agony with a strange dream.

CHAPTER 8

Hiram's Dream

Hiram Levy found himself suspended in a void. Below, replete with movement, a valley cautiously swirled into existence. Indiscernible shadows pushed and pulled, clamoring for their chance to *be*. Within the maelstrom, spotlights carved out the darkness, conjuring the famous Hollywood sign from empyrean firmament. "Why here?" Hiram wondered aloud. By autonomy alone, he floated closer and saw that the sign was illuminated by clunky, brightly lit words floating inside—movie star, celebrity, silver screen, epic, famous, fabulous, immortal, legend, superstar—with spatters of $ signs and *"ME"* intermingled among all of them. "...The cage that catches our dreams," he surmised.

Having unraveled the first act, his mind summoned a new muse: a gigantic and menacing red dragon, floating wistfully in and out of the clouds. The scales, the eyes, the tail, the fangs were all terrifying. Draped in a nefarious appearance, the beast spoke with a smooth, warm, world-class thespian tongue. "An actor's life for me! But wait—the theater has its demands—all must pay homage to the Grandest of Dragons. Only then will I get the red carpet treatment; only then will the crowd emerge. I, too, come from nowhere—pulled from obscurity. But, now I am some*where*, and I am some*body*." As Hiram struggled to stand fast against his fear of the dragon's incredible malevolence, adoring crowds bloomed from the ground itself. Slowly at first, like a record starting in the middle of a song, the onlookers began to call his name... "Hiram, Hiram, Hiram."

The scene changed. Hiram was standing on Hollywood Boulevard; before him, a square of wet cement with a dazzling gold star. The most beautiful women he had ever seen were in a cordon around him, arm in arm with the faces of yesterday's currency—Lincoln, Franklin, Grant, Jackson and Hamilton. All dressed in the finest modern attire, and all of them signaling their approval with raised glasses.

Hiram knew he was following a longstanding Hollywood tradition. Numerous movie stars came here to leave an imprint—a handprint, a footprint, a signature. In this place, where a kiss can bring a thousand dollars and a soul is given for fifty cents, Hiram wondered what his contribution would be. With his name proudly displayed in lights for the whole world to see, he felt compelled to leave something in the wet cement slab.

His guile took over. Struck with clarity, he realized it was all here... the fame, the wealth and the dragon in wait. All he had to do was kneel...acknowledge how wonderful this would all be.

But that was not Hiram. This was not his end game.

A sonic boom overshadowed his epiphany, terrifyingly capturing everyone's attention. Hitting the ground with a meteorite's velocity, yet none of its force, a massive cement slab inscribed with famous autographs landed and stretched effortlessly before him. Yet it was all still here...the crowd, the fabulous theatrics, the walk of fame, the autographs and the Hollywood elite. Without warning it all burst into nihility, the microscopic pieces consigned to insignificance.

Again, Hiram understood. This was a battle with the dragon. The recesses of his mind acknowledged his newfound cognizance, and his surroundings faded to black.

THE ELEPHANT

But a new scenario was born. White fog streamed into the darkness—finally, a transition that his conscious mind could account for.

A gargantuan space resembling an Olympic stadium, yet housing no athletic accoutrements, was gradually exposed. As Hiram's eyes adjusted, he recognized the enormous area was a stage. The haze was sucked further out toward the edges of the arena, revealing numerous giant elephants on the open field of the venue. They resembled steel, but possessed a spectacular luminosity that gave them the appearance of pure marble. Not unlike performing animals in a circus, they were comfortably seated and reaching toward the sky.

Hiram's eyes adjusted further, enabling him to focus on a man identical to himself standing atop one of the elephants. A hot air balloon emerged from the edge of the fog, carrying with it a group of rambunctious clowns. "Jump! Jump!" they called out. "We will catch you!"

"Hiram" held steady.

"Come on. You've got no faith in us? You can do this. You *know* who you are!" Their abhorrent jeering woke Hiram with a start, as if he had fallen and landed face-first into his concrete cell.

Back to the cold, immediate reality of prison. Hiram didn't even need to lift his head. The smell of the nearby cot, the chill of the damp air and the harsh frigid floor were stark reminders of his surroundings. But, there was something else. Footsteps? So it would seem. Glancing up, Hiram could make out a shadow advancing steadily along the corridor just outside the entrance to his cell.

There it was—the distinctive rattling of a large key ring. But, this was not the shadow of a well-armored prison guard. As the door slowly swung open, he could not believe Mei-ling's father was in front of him. No words were exchanged as Hiram accepted Shih's outreached arm. As they stood face-to-face, there was a pause as Hiram asked himself if he was actually awake. Captain Shih reached out, answering both Hiram's question and his prayers. They simply gripped each other by the arms in a strong embrace. More than mutual respect showed in their faces. There was an innate under-standing that they had been brought together.

CHAPTER 9

The Point of No Return

The days that followed Hiram's release proved more intense and frightening than anything he'd experienced in the military. The revelations were overwhelming. Shih spent hours poring over details of the Universal Order that confirmed Hiram's worst fears. Worldwide, people were being coerced and mobilized to operate at the will of a select few. They knew everything; they had manpower, weapons and surveillance that defied logic. They controlled everything. Shih had spent years meticulously recruiting and training a covert network, now operating across seven continents. But his pride and joy was his own North American cell—the 6 Trumpets. Shih's optimism did little to ease Hiram's despair in the face of such overwhelming odds. But he knew which side he was on; he knew it was now or never.

Less than a week after his discharge, Hiram found himself aboard an Airbus, accompanied by Captain Martin Shih, headed for McCarran International Airport just south of Las Vegas. Upon arrival, they were herded through their respective terminal with the rest of the flock to a monorail station where a rhythmic cadence of express trains shuttled newcomers to their final destination near the California-Nevada border—*The Theater of the Universal Order*.

The Greatest Celebration on Earth was how the colossal pageant had been billed—the 10th anniversary of the Order's *Manifesto* declaration and grand opening of the Theater. There was no hyperbole too great for this magnificent commencement. The Theater's construction had taken four years, during which it garnered notoriety as the architectural greeting to California's weekend warriors who made the high-speed burn through Baker and Barstow. They could see it for miles before arrival, thanks to the fabulous tower. The Eternity Tower...over 5,000 feet high. It was a structural *lusus naturae*, designed to create awe and wonder in all those fortunate enough to catch even a glimpse.

And then there was the titanic venue. Built to hold 250,000 souls, its song called out to the migratory nature of passport holders worldwide. This evening's event promised to be filled to maximum capacity. For those unable to attend, broadcast equipment around the tower was in the final stages of preparation to beam the extravaganza to the entire world.

Hiram and Martin's interest during their flight lay square on the impressive security at the facility. Remotely administered and monitored 24-7 from the Eastern seaboard by U.O. Headquarters in New York and augmented by a battalion of onsite armed guards on high alert, "safety" measures at today's event were built equally around psychology and pragmatism. Not only would the U.O. take no risks, they meant to instill prostration in weary travelers from the outset. For most, anticipation and excitement fended off the anxiety and consternation typical of tight crowds in close quarters. For Levy and Shih, a bit of jovial groupthink provided just the right kind of cover.

* * *

As the captain announced that the plane would be landing shortly, Hiram drew a deep breath and shifted his gaze out the windows to the sands below.

BACK TO NEVADA

It was time for his companion to make a subtle announcement of his own. Glancing casually at his smart watch, Shih sent a text message to Sergeant Bin-Ali, who was already in position on the ground. Abdul had been awaiting confirmation that Hiram and Shih were arriving on schedule and that their operation would initiate, as planned, at 1 p.m.—three hours before showtime.

Only seconds after pressing "Send," Captain Shih turned to Hiram with an unusually cold expression and said, "I want you to know that Mei-ling is part of today's operation." Previously free from anxiety in the face of the day's affairs, Hiram felt his heartbeat growing erratic.

"How?"

"Operation Delilah. She was a key part of staging some compromising conversations." Captain Shih sensed that Hiram was attracted to his daughter, and largely suspected the feeling was mutual.

"Will she be safe? I...I mean, will they go looking for her?" Hiram's words seemed to be running from him.

"No one on this mission is safe."

Martin's watch interrupted their conversation, trembling with life at a reply from Bin-Ali. The fasten seatbelt light illuminated, and Hiram felt a twinge of nausea as the plane descended. Landings didn't usually make him this uncomfortable, but he knew nothing would ever be the same after today.

Following the landing and mass exodus from McCarran's Terminal 3, Hiram and Captain Shih waited on the edge of the newly constructed Metro-Monorail Platform 24 for the next train to arrive. Shih, experienced in the art of surveillance, detected no signs of undercover pursuit by Transit Police or the Order. An eternity seemed to pass—unending minutes of discreetly checking the surrounding mob for disarray, hassle or danger. Relief swelled up as the next train careened into sight.

When the monorail doors slid open, Hiram and Shih broke for the compartment nearest to them. In surprisingly short order, a nasal but congenial voice came over the PA: "The doors are now closing." Temporarily reprieved from the thought of being followed, Captain Shih's attention focused on the weapons check they would face upon arrival at the stadium entrance—yet another delay. Hiram's attention wavered between the task at hand and the news of Mei-ling's involvement. "Will *this* be worth it?" he wondered in disgust. Although this time was different, his field experience made him loathe to risk any more lives—especially one as heartfelt as Mei-ling's. The train jolted into motion, signaling the irrelevance of his question and forcing him to accept the inevitable consequences which lay ahead.

* * *

Already on the ground, Bin-Ali was in the stadium's massive hangar, a structure placed adjacent to (but separate from) the auditorium proper. He was presently surrounded by a number of his fellow soldiers, members of the U.S. Army Corps of Engineers, most of whom were loyal to the U.O. They all had arrived in Las Vegas together, on orders to aid in finishing both the stadium and the hangar. Abdul fostered real relationships with many of them, and he prayed they would find forgiveness for, and understanding in, his actions.

Although officially designated a hangar, the facility appeared to have a singular purpose: a staging area for gigantic showpieces. Standing before the sergeant was a large group of steel elephants, standing on all fours, measuring six stories high and coated with polished gypsum alabaster. Leading the parade was one that appeared to be solid gold, seated on a pedestal and towering nine stories into the air. One of the young officers noticed his awe. "These fellas are going to be the highlight of tonight's show, sure to please young and old alike," he announced proudly, with no naiveté to speak of. He really seemed to believe.

Upon seeing blueprints for the "hangar" months earlier, a group of engineers developed misgivings about the design and subtly confided their suspicions to trusted officers. Why weren't there any windows? Why such a high ceiling? Why an extra layer of armed guards? It wasn't long before they found kinship with various Rangers who shared their sentiments, who trustingly revealed their intel on the Universal Order. With significant deliberation and months of planning, the group recruited former Ranger and newly minted Engineer Sergeant Bin-Ali, and five trusted souls of his choosing, to relay intelligence about the new construction project. Taking notes from the so-called terrorist playbook the U.O. had continually referenced in the weeks following the Nevada detonations, Abdul's sleeper cell worked side-by-side with troops loyal to the Universal Order.

The team was careful never to reveal their clandestine status, patiently waiting for contact from superiors whose identities were revealed only when necessary. Bin-Ali was the cell's point man, relaying details of the covert action through a maze of proxies and electronic aliases. Everyone on the team knew they were expendable, a fact they accepted when they signed up. The loss of one member would be insufficient to derail years of planning; the mission could *not* be abandoned under *any* circumstances.

* * *

At 1 p.m. Abdul and his team disbanded, each member silently working their way into the monstrous constructs of ego and greed via seamless hatches installed in secret during the beasts' construction. Over the next two hours, the cell implanted microscopic relays listening on an open channel to the Control Booth high above the spectator stands. The relays had a singular purpose: Upon waking, they would retransmit a live stream from the Control Booth to nearby amplifiers and speakers mounted at the base of each pachyderm. A sweep of the auditorium could happen at any time but the electronic tags listened passively, emitting no sign of their existence until stirred by a digital key.

From the audience's distant perspective, the elephants would appear to deliver a series of spoken messages to a full house. Such theatrics and puppetry lay at the heart of the operation—a counterpoint to the Order's pronouncements of peace and prosperity, laid bare by their own instruments.

The only unresolved part of the entire operation was the second phase. The question remained: How to get the team—without being detected—up and into the Control Booth so the operatives could transmit? Variables were plentiful; solutions were in short supply. Even after gaining access to the booth, the position would have to be defended while the operation continued.

Sergeant Bin-Ali had been the Chief Engineer assigned to oversee the installation of video surveillance throughout the venue. He knew that the wiring for the hangar was separate from that of the auditorium—including its security cameras. The main circuit breaker for the hangar's lighting was located in the basement, an unguarded area which the original architects (incorrectly) thought would require no surveillance. The time Abdul spent building the hangar taught him everything about the surveillance and lighting systems, allowing him to manipulate them at will.

With only 40 minutes left on the clock and concealed in the last-minute confusion typical of any large-scale production, Bin-Ali slipped down an unguarded staircase toward the basement. On a previous visit he had already sabotaged the auxiliary lighting system. The only thing left was to cut the power to the main circuit breakers and insert a short obfuscation into the hangar's video feed.

The sergeant had prepared a laptop and custom software specifically assembled to intercept the IP-based video camera feed. Popping open the network cabinet, and taking a single deep breath, he pulled the Ethernet cable from the network switch aggregating the hangar's cameras and swapped it with his laptop's connection. Any monitoring sensors would surely detect a brief delay, but engineering school taught him that minute periods of unresponsiveness were the norm for any network where cables ran in excess of 2,000 miles.

Abdul finally exhaled. His custom application indicated there was now a 60-minute recording of this morning's events looping smoothly back in New York.

Confident that his sensors rang true, he moved on to the hangar's lighting. With the flip of a switch, the basement was shrouded in darkness. Within seconds, he heard generators kick in to restore minimal lighting to the hangar itself. But the brief confusion was all they needed—a contingent of rebel forces had already infiltrated the hangar, posing as drivers tasked with delivering the main attractions to the Theater. The flickering lights were the signal they had been waiting for.

As Abdul sprinted up the stairs, shots rang out sporadically. The heavy soundproof hangar doors concealed the charge, assuming no loyalist breached the emergency exits. The sergeant had full confidence in his allies, and rightfully so. With the precision of a well-rehearsed symphony, every resistant U.O. guard was subdued; in some cases with extreme prejudice.

By the time Bin-Ali emerged from the stairwell, the fight was already over. Letting his eyes adjust to the dim emergency lighting, Abdul glibly absorbed the scene before ordering the casualties gagged and moved to a nearby elephant—the one embossed with an American flag. When the head lifted upward, allowing easy access to the interior, the sergeant felt a twinge of disbelief that he had coordinated such a move against his own comrades. "Make them comfortable," he barked at the Rangers tending to the wounded.

In case the Control Booth could not be taken, or if the signal transmitted from it failed to reach the relays, a backup system was designed. Its components were strewn about small compartments within the elephant's interior; every operative had the assembly process memorized. Also stored within the elephant was a small USB drive holding a number of videos copied from U.O. Headquarters by Shih's connections. The drive was to be inserted into the Order's holographic projector inside the Theater—a giant display originally intended to be the opening act for the pachyderm parade. Captain

Shih and Hiram had different plans in mind for the evening's meg-alomaniacal display. Thanks to a production of their own, tonight *they* would appear before all the spectators (and the world).

The elephant's head was lowered back into place and sealed. Twenty minutes had passed—10 minutes from now, a small contingent would be arriving to escort the elephants the short distance to the Theater. Bin-Ali's comrades quickly traded their uniforms for those worn by captive guards. This was the key. The bold masquerade granted them unfettered access to the Control Booth. Once the elephants were in position, accompanied by a discreet selection of small arms, they would take the freight elevator to the Control Booth and push reality into the limelight...

CHAPTER 10

The Greatest Show on Earth

The Metro-Monorail terminal was over a mile away from the grand arena, but even from that distance the structure was beyond impressive—it was imposingly overwhelming. The arena stood 20 stories high with a circumference of more than a mile. The monorail passengers stepped into sweltering desert heat as they filled the boarding platforms. From there, scores of smaller stadium trolleys would whisk excited spectators to their exact gate destination— hundreds at a time. Transportation personnel checked each person who got on the trolleys for lanyards and ID tickets. It was quite an elaborate system. When their trolley showed up, Hiram and Captain Shih were among the first passengers to climb aboard. The air-conditioned coach provided a cool mobile oasis from the hot, arid environment outside.

The trolleys filled in no time, and departed briskly. Within five minutes they easily covered the distance to the Theater of the Universal Order. By now it was past 3 p.m. Fortunately, the normally blistering, afternoon sky was overcast, making the short walk from the trolley station platform to the arena's entrance a little more tolerable; at least the sun wasn't beating down on anyone. The arena was fitted with a massive domed roof that could open and close depending on the season or time of day. Artificial darkness could be created at any time to stage light shows with lasers, or the latest in performance technology—giant holographic projections—as would be the case with today's presentation.

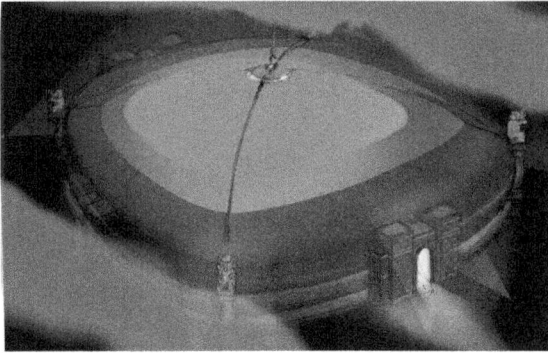

After the security delay through the initial entrance for an obligatory weapons check, the spectators sauntered to extra-wide moving walkways. The rolling esplanades carried them to impressively steep escalators, which delivered them to smaller moving walkways, efficiently transporting each and every spectator to the entrance of their respectively assigned seats. At each transfer point, high-speed scanners double- and triple-checked the ticket holders. The show was set to start at 4 p.m. sharp and there would be a full house. This was, after all, the "Spectacular Spectacle of Grand Openings."

As Hiram and Shih ascended to the upper tiers in one of the high-rise escalators, they watched in muted awe as the dimensions of the facilities unfolded below and around them. The drawings and surveillance photos paled in comparison to actually experiencing the monument. Their seats were located on the third tier. Exiting at this level, they noted that the stadium was already half-full. Thousands of waiting spectators were passing the time by watching videos on a number of huge screens positioned beneath the massive shaded dome above their heads. It was already 3:30 p.m. and thousands of men, women and children were still taking their seats. Top U.O. officials were just now settling into the Theater in loges located high atop the reviewing stands. Naturally, they would have the best view in the house. Meanwhile, vendors were doing their part to keep the crowds occupied by handing out complimentary refreshments.

Captain Shih gently elbowed his fellow conspirator. "Can you believe it—a quarter of a million people all here," he exclaimed. "Just imagine a riot breaking out..." Presently, Hiram lifted his eyes upward and to the left. Pointing in that direction, he got the captain's attention, "Look up there, Martin." The captain turned his head to the left and scanned the VIP section located adjacent to the Control Booth. There, within one of the glass-enclosed loges—it looked like a grandiose theater box—was what appeared to be a large throne, standing empty in the middle of the room with lighting on both sides. Neither of the two men could make sense of this. "Well," grinned Hiram, "just more proof that the U.O. is suffering from delusions of grandeur."

The anticipation grew. Both men checked their watches—almost showtime. And then, ever so gradually, the looping clips on the big screens faded to black and silence descended upon all 250,000 visitors as the house lights dimmed. On cue, the crowd settled into anticipation, waiting for something wonderful to begin. The long-awaited extravaganza was about to commence.

Distinct notes of symphonic strings slowly rose to audible levels. The sound floated in from every direction. It was unlike any symphony the world had ever heard. As pinpoint lighting effects danced across the undersurface of the darkened dome, the music rose to a crescendo. An intricate pattern of laser lights wove a delicate web in midair as a light, smoky haze appeared.

Soon the scattered laser lights began to converge, producing a mammoth three-dimensional image. The holographic projection didn't even require a screen; it seemed to simply hang in thin air. There, before the entire amazed crowd, stood a man larger than life dressed in top hat and tails—the Master of Ceremonies. Smiling, he stood against a background of orange, white and green—the color scheme of the whole auditorium. Surrounding him was a mist of fine crystals—a dead giveaway that this was a 3D holographic projection. It was a spectacular illusion of an illusion. Yet, the man seemed so real standing there, smiling at a quarter of a million real faces before him—and billions more through TV screens and monitors around the world.

"Ladie---s and gen---tlemen, for your pleasure and entertainment on this auspicious occasion, we bring you an extravaganza never before seen on earth." The audience erupted into thunderous applause and exuberant cheers.

As the tumult died down, the Master of Ceremonies began again. The image of him zoomed to a close-up. In the enduring style of an old-time circus ringmaster, the distinguished impresario spoke again: "You, my friends, are about to witness the greatest spectacle of all time. This is the Procession of Humanity.... Ah, but you ask, 'From where shall such a grand procession begin? Where are the backdrops, the scenery, the stage?' Just wait! All is here through the wonder of technology!

"And no," continued the orator, "there are no miracles here—certainly not—and no magic... Science has put an end to all that. But...illusions? Well, what do your eyes tell you...?"

As he spoke, the Master of Ceremonies dissolved, vanishing from sight. But a new image appeared seconds later in the form of a beautiful, young Chinese woman in a white silk gown—speaking in a lovely soprano voice. "As you see," she said demurely, "nothing is impossible for Man, or for that matter, Woman."

Again the crowd roared its approval in astonished laughter. She continued, "And now, ladies and gentlemen, without further ado, I give you the first celebration of the Universal Order!"

She stretched forth her graceful arm in a wide, sweeping gesture...

"Ancient Babylon."

A fresh mist of microscopic crystals blew into the huge central area of the arena, forming the necessary matrix for an ever larger colossal holographic display. Instantly, the crowd was transported through time and space to the King's Court of Ancient Babylon. The spectators became part of an immense wall running the perimeter of the stadium. 3D chariots passed along the parapets of the wall high above their heads. Mighty horses, their hooves beating in time to ancient music, ran along the upper level circumference of the great Theater. Hanging gardens appeared, green and alive and so real they looked like each person could reach out and touch. The actual fragrance of flowers swayed in the artificial breeze that blew rapturous scents throughout the room.

The scene unfolding on the palace grounds far below was displayed on the arena's video screens, playing out like an old silent film. Hundreds of merchants, soldiers and peasants visited the marketplace just outside the palace. Within, the beautiful young Queen of Babylon, accompanied by her pet leopard, leaned her head against the King's knee while sitting at the foot of his throne. His visage was that of a gracious and loving king—the true image of human virtue—a good man.

The beautiful Chinese woman appeared again, "Behold…the King of Babylon—but honored by his own people—a paragon of virtue—a true Humanist! His advisors were astronomers—men of science. And civilization begins!" Again, applause broke out from the Spectators' Gallery.

"Now my fellow citizens, we continue with our 10 years' celebration of the Universal Order's Manifesto—that much respected declaration of tolerance. While Babylon now sleeps, we open a path in history for the Parade of Man. Witness his many accomplishments! In the face of false and oppressive mythology, and age-old superstition, behold what man, aided by science and reason, has accomplished!"

Suddenly, the Chinese woman vanished into thin air, and along with her the entire Babylonian scenario.

The next scene unfolded to an old woman kneeling in shadows, enveloped by a nearly transparent silken cocoon. Her features were tired and worn; her clothes, tattered and stained. She was a picture of hopelessness. Most of the spectators sat in a slight state of discomfort. What was the message here?

The deep voice of the Ringmaster rang out: "Behold—see how the Universal Order has transformed our world." With that, the viewing cloud flashed to illuminate the old woman within the cocoon from the inside out. For a few brief seconds, she literally glowed.

And then it started.

Magically, as she rose to her feet, she was transformed into a beautiful, young geisha, dressed in a traditional flowered kimono. The ruptured cocoon fragments dissolved and transformed into a cloud of colorful butterflies. Smiling, this elegant, reborn geisha revealed her half-hidden face from behind a paper fan. As she swept the fan in a wide arc above her head, the butterflies were gently pushed out into the audience, where some of them appeared to rest on the heads of the spectators. Amazed children reached out to catch these illusive phantoms, only to come up empty-handed. The magic of it fascinated the all-ages crowd, prompting laughter, amazement and applause.

The geisha and her winged entourage floated from view. A new segment was ready to commence. A vast blue canopy appeared above the heads of the crowd, while clouds drifted serenely by. Below, on the central, broad floor area, a stream babbled through a beautiful garden. Distant snow-capped mountains decorated the background. In the foreground, partially obscured by flowers and shrubs, stood a man and woman. Some even guessed they were the mythical Adam and Eve. A polite round of applause accompanied the enchanting re-creation of the Garden of Eden fairytale.

But the mood shifted. An ominous sound echoed through the huge venue. Monstrous shadows arose. It appeared. A dragon entered, slinking through this paradise in all his serpent-like splendor! His beauty was surpassed only by his cunning visage. The audience followed his movements with rapt fascination—as if the ancient spell still had the power to entice.

Without warning, everything became a blur of human history. The stunning visuals literally flew the audience through centuries of time to the Industrial Age. The Ringmaster narrated as incredible images flew by, one era fading into the next....

"True," he expounded, "the natural world has its beauty...but so, too, does the world of modern technology—the gleam of metal, the rhythm of the powerful engine and the genius design of the integrated circuit. All of this belongs to our modern age. La---die---sssss and gen---tle---men, I give you the March of the Robots."

As the spectators directed their attention to the lower level of this vast arena, a parade of gleaming robots—mechanical men, mechanized pack animals, mobile units of all shapes and sizes— marched across the floor of the stadium as an airborne flotilla of drones buzzed around in the air above them. The future was now. "These creatures," proclaimed the commentator, "are all fashioned by their creator—Man."

The audience applauded his comments. These machines, like the previous participants in the show, were magnified as holographic images.

Following the March of the Robots came the March of the Flags of Nations. This was a spectacularly colorful display, again gaining energetic approval from the crowd. The flags were arranged in symmetrical patterns, and gradually lowered until in the midst of them arose a giant flag of the Universal Order. Instinctually, everyone rose to their feet, singing along to a stirring rendition of the Universal Anthem, "Hail, Great Unconquered Human Spirit."

But the parade marched on, the next scenario brandishing the benefits promised by the latest developments in cryobiology—cryogenic stasis, an alternative offered to citizens reaching the age of 85 years. An elderly man and woman, perhaps a married couple, were peacefully led to their cryogenic chambers by a friendly cryotech assistant. They entered the chambers in joy, laying horizontal for the process to begin.

They remained at peace.

The scene transitioned to a close-up of a digital clock which proceeded to show the passage of time over the years. The years flew by in seconds, showcasing the miracle of technology. At the end of "The Metamorphosis of Science Solutions," the two were revived, looking no older than when they had entered the chambers years earlier. But now, they awakened to a future world in which humanity possessed the scientific means for giving them back their youth, "a rejuvenating technology"! The sequence's finale thrust the two back into the prime of their life, holding hands as they disappeared from view. The audience was inspired and deeply moved.

"We now see eternity within our grasp. We no longer need to believe myths to have hope in the future!"

The crowd roared in approval and the pageant moved into the next act.

"We stand in hope now, united as human beings in our government, our economies, our safety and our faiths," the announcer proclaimed. "Allow me to introduce our spiritual leaders—all united in a pact to live, worship and walk the world in peace."

On cue, religious leaders marched across the floor of the arena in ranks, six abreast. Throughout the long marching line were brilliant banners, which bore the inscriptions, "Peace," "Brotherhood," "Love," "Acceptance" and "Tolerance." As each group entered they were magnified into holographic images. Looking around at all the spectators, they couldn't help but notice the approving smiles and encouraging applause. Then, in unison, they shouted out, "Hatred is the enemy of Tolerance." It was obvious, tolerance was the prime directive—whether in religious life, social life or political life. It was just that simple—tolerance was the key to peace.

The religious leaders' words, echoing from the arena's loudspeakers, were greeted by a standing ovation.

Following the parade of the world's religious leaders, who, in reality, were merely tolerated by the new regime, the voice of the Ringmaster rang out again. "And now—citizens of the world—allow us to continue our illumination. As you know, technology is reshaping our world...making it better, richer and safer. But ultimate safety would mean a world without crime, correct...? Well, I ask you: If one's conscience is deemed insufficient to control habitual misbehavior, despite our sincerest efforts to reform, what alternative do we have?"

There was a rhetorical pause.

"*Technology!* Yes, in the near future, with the aid of a new techno-logical process, we will actually be able to determine the thoughts of *anyone* previously incarcerated for a specific crime. Observe...."

CHAPTER 11

An End to Crime

Once again, a hologram appeared before the spectators that showed a rapidly moving series of images. They were old mug shots of criminals, but as the clip moved along the pictures grew increasingly modern.

"In the past, one of the most consistent facts regarding crime is that criminals will almost always become repeat offenders. Since locating the nerve center of criminal psychographics, it's only logical to identify them for the common good and safety of all."

As these words were uttered, a final photo floated into focus and zoomed in to display a close-up of an inmate in modern garb. But there was one difference—glowing, red eyes.

"Notice this man's red eyes. No, he hasn't caught the early morning express to Chicago. His eyes have turned red because he has recently had 'violent or angry' thoughts! A small implant at the base of his skull is capable of reading his neuro-electric patterns; in essence, his thoughts. In turn, the implant sends a color signal to the iris of the man's eyes. In the near future, all prisoners guilty of

specific, dangerous crimes will be implanted with these microchips. Thanks to the color of their eyes, anyone will be able to spot them *before* they harm or insult another person! The colors have significance...red in the case of anger, bright green in the case of sexual assault and, most importantly, yellow in the case of intolerance. Anyone with a smart phone can immediately notify authorities with an alarm. Their identity will be tied to the GPS area of the phone alert, facilitating immediate arrests.

"And with this system we will implement the long-awaited 'Three Strikes' program, enabling us to humanely limit treacherous personalities from harming society any further," proudly proclaimed the Ringmaster.

Another hologram appeared. Three men were standing in a police lineup. Two of these men clearly had normal eyes, while a third man's eyes, a priest, brightly shone yellow. The Ringmaster continued, "Now, you don't have to be a law officer to figure this one out, do you.... Who is the intolerant one?"

After a brief pause, the audience answered him, as if they were reading from a script. "The priest!" they cried. Someone with a loud voice near the front stood up shaking his fist screaming, "The bastard in the frock!"

"And what will we do with him?" asked the Ringmaster.

Again the audience answered in frenzied unison: "Freeze him! Freeze him! Freeze him," they chanted.

With that the image disappeared, only to be replaced by a close-up of the Ringmaster. "The jury has spoken," he whispered. The audience applauded wildly at the matrimony of technological innovation and judicial efficiency.

CHAPTER 12

The Parade of the Elephants

"We certainly hope you have enjoyed this first portion of our celebration—but the evening is far from over! Now we transport you beyond the earth itself! Not content with conquering earth and all its resources, man has always looked beyond his own planet. And in his quest, he has reached for the stars. Gaze upon our latest conquest!"

The audience gasped as a marble of gas and dust transmuted into the planet Saturn, its rings floating well into the stands. For a moment, the spectators actually felt as if they were floating on the colorful, gossamer rings. Laughter and wonderment filled the arena. In the midst of this magical orbit, a satellite swung into view. As it continued its smooth orbit about the planet, the spectators could clearly see the emblem of the Universal Order Space Agency stamped on the side. "Behold," exclaimed the Ringmaster, "we have given Saturn a new moon."

Hiram became enraged at the hubris of such a grandiose statement. But his anger quickly turned to laughter at such foolish pride.
Recalling Emerson's words, he smiled:

"For what are they all in their high conceit, when man in the bush
with God may meet?"

Hiram had met his God a long time ago and was at peace with what
he believed was an eternal truth.

And now the extravaganza, with all its pomp and splendor, was nearing its climax. With rousing fanfare, the grand finale rolled through the entryway. The Parade of the Elephants—seven spectacular animatronic elephants, representing each of the new Continental Coalitions, drifting majestically on monstrous floats.

The spectators could hardly believe their eyes as they watched these mammoths effortlessly glide to their assigned places around the perimeter of the stadium floor. Standing on all fours, the elephants reached a height of six stories. Taking in the spectacle, Hiram bela-

bored the obvious, "Just like the proverbial 'White Elephant'—an unwanted gift that you can't unload on anyone else—sounds like the U.O. itself." On each flank, prominently displayed for everyone to see, were the various flags of what had become the world's seven major nation states.

As the citizens of each represented continent nation spotted the emblem of their own country, they raised a loud, rallying cheer. With all their enthusiasm, cheer and antics, the spectators had become the biggest cast of extras in the history of show business. So far, the show had certainly lived up to its name: The Greatest Celebration on Earth. Of course, it had all been staged to present the Universal Order in the best possible light.

The spectators' participation only added to the showmanship—audiences around the world celebrated in their own spectacular ways.

The processional of elephants made three complete passes around the arena in harmony with a fabulous music and light show, complete with perfectly timed pyrotechnics. It finally came to a halt with all of the elephants perfectly spaced around the arena floor. In the center towered the Master of Ceremonies, the Ringmaster, in a six-story-tall hologram. His amplified voice soaring above the roar of the crowd, he announced, "Ladie---s and gen---tlemen, I give you the Universal Order." With the echo of his decree still reverberating throughout the arena, he once again vanished.

THE GOLDEN ELEPHANT

With the arena in near total darkness, only a gradually ascending fanfare of trumpets signaled the show was not over. Everyone jumped to their feet with a round of applause. A sudden burst of activity off to the west caught the crowd's attention. What they saw was nothing less than stupendous: a marvelous golden elephant seated on a pedestal and draped with a purple robe was making its way into the arena. Three stories taller than the others, its diamond-studded ivory tusks projected forward 40 feet. Embossed on either side of the lavender vestment was the image of a golden dragon...the new symbol of the Universal Order. The golden beast was paraded along the spectator stands, passing along the outside edge of the stationary smaller elephants; they now seemed so insignificant compared to this monster. This colossal effigy concluded its victory lap with a grand entrance to the center of the arena. Somehow, the music always seemed to get louder—more grandiose...

As the sublimely beautiful mammoth sat imposingly at the center of attention, trumpets blared once again. A clap of thunder descended from the center of the ceiling, calling everyone's attention upward. As if he had materialized by will alone, a flying acrobat swooped down, propelled through the air by a jetpack. Trailing behind was the flag of the Universal Order. The crowd, still on its feet, grew quiet as the people pledged solemnity to the flag. After brazenly circling the capacity audience, the daredevil landed gently on top of the golden elephant's head.

This was the cue for Hiram and Captain Shih to take action.

Quickly leaving their seats, Captain Shih walked briskly toward the Control Booth, where a rebel contingent lay in wait. Hiram made his way to the lower level of the arena and headed for the American elephant.

The house lights were lowered and the spectators returned to sitting. The Theater's audio-visual system again suffused the senses with a beautifully synchronized music and laser display. But, in less than a minute, a disconcerting screech resounded through every corner of the arena. Both the lighting and PA went dead. Silence followed as emergency house lights restored a

THE PARADE OF THE ELEPHANTS

modicum of visibility. The crowd's abstruse whispers hung low in the air—surely *this* was not part of the show. Everyone expected an apologetic announcement—but none came.

Catching the crowd off-guard, two men appeared side-by-side before all 250,000 spectators and viewers around the world. The holograms rivaled the Ringmaster at an incredible 10 stories tall, their presence filling the arena. Their pre-recorded message introduced them simply as Hiram Levy, now a civilian and a former U.S. Army Ranger, and Captain Shih, a U.S. Navy Seal. Captain Shih's likeness concluded their appearance with the following: "Our mission here today is to invite you, the people, to simply come, listen and see truth for yourself. As the great American patriot Thomas Paine once said: 'But such is the irresistible nature of truth, that all it asks, and all it wants, is the liberty of appearing.'"

The Ringmaster scurried to contact the Control Booth via headset. After only a few panicked seconds, he realized his cries were going unheard. Someone was jamming his transmitter! He had no other recourse but to address the audience with the PA. His voice rang out across the auditorium: "Somebody, please cut the satellite feed. Stop the transmission!" But someone in the Control Booth had stealthily disabled the manual override; no one could pull the plug.

And the whole world was watching.

CHAPTER 13

A Conspiracy of Clowns

PROFIT IN THE DEATH INDUSTRY

The crowd sat in silence as 10 stories of light flashed a new scene: a group of senior U.O. officials with Henry Varick at the helm. As Varick began to speak, his voice seemed to be emanating from the elephant emblazoned with the United States flag. His delivery no longer consisted of the smooth, congenial tone so familiar to the public. The words were sharp, with an edge of condescension. Greed and matter-of-fact prudence leaked from between the syllables. The conversation's tone was casual but cavalier; he appeared to be leading a staff meeting.

Even with your eyes closed, you could hear the words whistling through a grin.

"With the world's population rapidly aging, we're looking at an annual market potential of one hundred million elderly reaching the age of

85. Add to that, nearly 30 million handicapped children under the age of 10. Of course, for the aged, this procedure will be mandatory; but for the handicapped youngsters the *choice* will be made by their parents. We've developed a cost-effective technology to stave off decomposition. And as long as we don't have to invest in cures or safe thaw processes, then this is a sustainable and extremely profitable business model."

Dr. Rebecca Walker, Director of the International Health Cooperative, protested immediately. "You mean to tell me that there is no plan to invest any of the designated profits into R&D?" She was on the edge of shock. "That's unconscionable!"

As Henry Varick anticipated, Walker and her young assistant stormed out in disgust at the revelation. The remaining medical representatives looked nervous. When the door sealed behind the two women, a short, nervous man tried to assuage his own guilt, "Well, you've got to be tough in this business...and keep it *business*," he emphasized. "If you take it personal, someone else will take your profits."

Patience was sucked out of the arena, the betrayal launching a shocked and angry crowd to their feet in disapproval. The reel played on, uninterested in the crowd's opinion.

"Speaking of profits, cryotech likely holds an annual market of $50 billion. Not too shabby—would you agree, folks?" Non-verbal approvals were unanimous. Henry Varick smugly nodded.

The disturbing boardroom scene on the giant panorama seamlessly dissolved from view, replaced by one of the Universal Order's cryogenic facilities. The sheer vastness of neatly rowed "eternity pods" was staggering in and of itself, and this was just one of many facilities in each state. But the camera didn't stop with the wide shot, relentlessly revealing in quick succession window after window of grotesque, zombie-like sleeping men, women and children. Gasps of horrified enlightenment escaped from the audience—their own aging parents and relatives, as well as sick and handicapped children, had been trustingly released into such chambers. A hoax of hope had been unmasked.

But the footage continued, relentlessly chipping away at the public's faith. The audience was now subjected to a thin, frosty-haired cryo-technician leading a small girl from the anteroom through two double doors toward the stasis chambers. With her parents waving in the distance, the technician gently hugged the little limping girl and asked in a sweet whisper, "Now Katie, didn't you have fun at the amusement park today?" She nodded with a cute smile as she turned to the guide from waving back to her folks and blurted out, "Oh, it was so much fun that I wish it would have never ended." The tech's trembling voice betrayed his confident facade. "Well, we're not finished yet. We've saved the best ride for last..."

Beyond a set of pneumatic doors in the processing lab was a second technician, a busy, beefy woman, on hand to monitor the procedure. She didn't turn around, not even to glance at who was entering the chamber. "It's *cold* in here," exclaimed Katie, as she began to shiver. With the finish line in sight, the technician doubled down on the charade. "Don't worry, it's just special effects. Hop onto the platform and I'll strap you in. This is going to be the ride of your life!"

"Hurry, it's getting colder!" cried the little girl as she scurried into the glass casket. The male gave a quiet sigh of relief while his burly colleague verified temperature, vitals and scheduling. As vapors began to circulate about her face, Katie's happy expression twisted to one of excruciating distress.

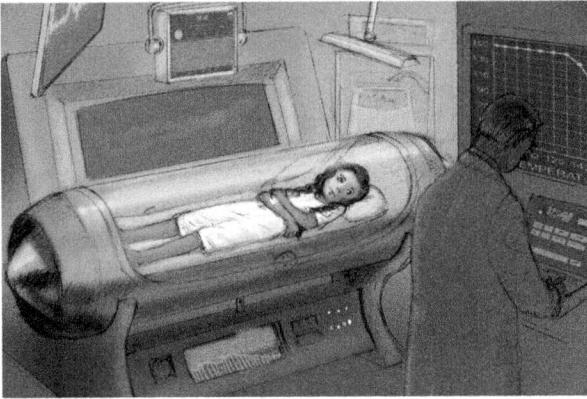

The VIP section rose to their feet in confused outrage at their total lack of control over the situation. Their section, a theater loge high above the arena floor, commanded a clear view of this embarrass- ment. The loge was equipped with a separate PA system originally intended for making "personalized" addresses to the audience. Fred Hamson, a senior cabinet member, was outraged. He grabbed the microphone: "Stop the broadcast—immediately. Kill the sound... kill the sound!" The audio-visual crew scurried, trying to trace the source of the incoming AV signal. Meanwhile, two or three detach- ments of the U.O. security guards had already scattered across the field at the center of the arena. They began searching the tiers of spectators, looking for any indication of the signal's origin. It was a

Sisyphean task—there were 250,000 attendees!

Down below, the U.S. elephant projecting the audio was now surrounded by an anxious guard detachment. The drawn weapons did little to shield their looks of confusion and fear. But the elephant had now fallen silent, collapsing the holographic image with it and leaving nothing behind but an angry crowd. One intrepid guardsman asked a desperate question to his commander, "Are they telling us to 'kill it down', sir?" The officer retorted, "Shoot it?!? It ain't even alive!"

No sooner had his words escaped than *another* animatronic beast took to pantomiming Henry Varick. His adoption as the most hated official of the U.O. marched on in another excerpt from a devastating highlight reel. With half the world watching, "The Greatest Show on Earth" was devolving into "The Greatest Humiliation on Earth."

TERRORISM

Having appeared frequently before television audiences around the world, the scar on the right side of his face made Varick easily recognizable to the crowd. His voice was incredibly clear as it came through the giant animal puppet, addressing a U.O. governing council.

Exclaiming with his hands in the air, "The public won't bail out our banks this time. We can't make growth happen; we're stuck in this hole of a nuclear depression. The only chance we have of salvaging the global economy is to press the reset button. I mean for the entire globe! The whole operation has to be shut down, and we can get it restarted by shutting down the power grid. The world is overleveraged again. The dollar's collapse is imminent and China won't stand for it—they'll support our plan rather than see their holdings of U.S. treasuries collapse!"

Dismay set in as spectators tried to reconcile the reassuring man they saw each evening during the global blackout, with the sociopath ranting before them now. Three nights in a row he had claimed that the U.O. was making great sacrifices to restore just enough power for his nightly broadcasts. He guaranteed the public that the U.O. had the situation well in hand and would regain control of the grid within the next few days. He had made it clear that he was speaking for both the Universal Order Administration and for the 10 major nations, including the United States, that continued to resist the terrorist element.

Until this very moment, most of the world had been taken in by his theatrics of sincerity in the midst of a crisis—but now? Well, he was just getting warmed up.

"The public is incredibly gullible and deep down inside they are afraid—the complexities of real economic and political issues are way over their heads. Tell 'em the sky is falling and the boogey man is coming...they'll believe it!

"So what's the key? *Terrorism!* They think terrorists are capable of *anything.* All we have to do is claim that this was all the work of some terrorists and the public will buy it. It's up to us to bail out the world, right? That makes *us* the heroes here. Yes, you are hearing me correctly, *terrorists* can be our allies here."

His fervor continued. "We can spread rumors like WMDs are floating around out there, but tell the folks that the U.O. has crack commandos and special intelligence units to track them down. As a matter of fact, this is precisely what we did in Nevada. We can actually create and control a crisis to present it in the best possible light to the media—simply put, here's how we saved you and your city. But it gets better—we can leverage the crisis to suspend the burden of certain laws. The fact is we need this kind of flexibility to govern more effectively during emergencies. Hell, it's for their own good!"

Both of the talking elephants were now surrounded by security details. The Ringmaster hysterically, frantically, shouted out contradictory commands. First, he gave the order, "Shoot the damn elephants!" The guards opened fire. The statues took inconsequential damage, but nearby civilians were not so fortunate. Disorder within the crowd shifted to wholesale panic. The Ringmaster backpedaled, screaming, "Stop, you idiots—you'll get us all killed!" The troops obeyed, taking a nervous stance as the crowd's animosity flowed downhill toward mob mentality aimed directly at anything that resembled organized authority.

The Ringmaster, now certain the situation had passed the tipping point, grabbed an ostensibly functional radio from a nearby guard.

"This is Center Stage One: To all guard units—evacuate *all* VIPs—repeat—evacuate all VIPs. We've gotta shut down these damn elephants!

"Airstrike authorized on my position!"

CHAPTER 14

Behind the Masks of Power

OPERATION DELILAH

The crowd seemed to sulk into submissive observation, exhausted by the non-stop barrage on their worldview. What could possibly come next? A third elephant, sporting the Asian Union flag, answered in the voice of Harold J. Randolph, Secretary of Federal Communications—another governmental celebrity. The latest segment placed him as the romantic lead in an elegant milieu, engaged in conversation with a shapely, beautiful woman half his age. Mei-ling! The two were sitting in a private section of an upscale restaurant. She was wearing a designer dress that accented all her best features, and, of course, a pair of stiletto heels that showcased her spectacular pins.

As Hiram watched the sequence unfold, he experienced regret and anguish evolving into rage. Mei-ling was so beautiful—and he loved this brave, young woman so much. She had played her part perfectly in this setup...and now she was little more than bait—probably finished. If the U.O. emerged intact after the evening's events, their revenge for this "treachery" would follow her all the way to death's door. Hiram prayed that, at this moment, she was somewhere safe.

In recent weeks everyone had seen Randolph's handsome face on television promoting the Universal Order's "safe communication protocols"—thinly veiled attempts to use national security issues to justify more censorship and control. He never missed a chance to push family values and the importance of protecting children. Perhaps his colleagues had placed too much trust in such an arrogant cynic. His distinguished good looks and gregarious nature, which had initially helped him appeal to the common man, had ultimately turned out to be a double-edged sword. He liked to smile at charming companions as he boasted about his accomplishments. It always worked, and this scene was a classic...

"These kids just don't know what's going on. If they only knew that they're being used. We've made a helluva lot of money off their purchasing power, thanks to market research," he winked. He leveraged the moment of flippancy to gently caress her delicate arm.

Mei-ling smiled wonderfully.

"This younger generation in particular is addicted to mobile devices. We know what makes 'em tick, because we know what they *text!*" As he chuckled about his power, his hand playfully came down a little more confidently on hers. Her hand did not move, rather she gently embraced his between her thumb and the side of her index finger.

Randolph leaned in focusing his steel blue eyes intently into Mei-ling's beautiful face. Her rich, brown, innocent eyes held his gaze. "Ya' know, the key to marketing, where these young people are concerned anyway, is to appeal to their vanity. You've got to pander to their romantic illusions using cheap thrills and sex. Sex sells," he purred mischievously, inching a bit closer as he deftly maneuvered his hand to brush lightly across her bare back. Her spiked heel softly nudged his leg.

"Yes, it does," giggled his glamorous dinner companion, leaning just a little closer as if trying to capture his immense "wisdom" all for herself. "This is fascinating! I had no idea..."

Self-assured, his incriminations showed no sign of slowing.

"Take their lifestyle, for instance. They actually *think* we admire their non-conformity. In reality, *they* are conformers...to *our* programming. *We* call the shots and pull their strings. *We're* telling *them* what they *think* they want. If they knew the simple truth, they'd know the Pied Piper they dance to is just an old, white-haired V.P. who works for me. He doesn't give a damn about them," he said as they both leaned together, bursting into laughter. Their faces ended up just inches from each other now as their eyes locked into that...gaze. Randolph grinned devilishly while raising his glass for a long sip. He paused, allowing the vodka to take hold. Mei-ling's lips were more inviting with every drink. Another pause and then Randolph leaned in ravenously, his right hand softly caressing her thigh. Hiram no longer hated this man—he now loathed him. This was a man who once had a daughter about Mei-ling's age, before cancer took her.

This image softly faded with Randolph groping the Asian beauty, leaving spectators feeling like stunned voyeurs. Many couldn't accept the fact that they'd been so easily duped—by philanderers and liars whom they had actually grown to admire. It was incredibly uncomfortable to see a respected leader so lustily and candidly seducing a young woman. "What was he thinking? I can't believe he fell for this. 'No fool like an old fool,' is what Grandma used to say," Hiram said to no one in particular.

On the ground around the elephants, total chaos was grabbing the reins one hand at a time. No one had thought of the simplest solution: Remove these mechanical pachyderms from the arena. Inexplicably, the "drivers" had disappeared. A contingent of *real* U.O. guards abandoned the elephants and piled into a service elevator, which took them to the large Control Booth high above the stadium.

As the doors opened, the guards rushed out toward the entrance to the booth. Weapons drawn, they were greeted by a complement of well-prepared Navy Seals and Army Rangers. The rebels were accosted with a hail of insults and ultimatums from the U.O.

regime's soldiers. Unfazed by the verbal assaults, Shih's contingent stood firm against the Order's guards—but there was no exchange of gunfire.

A WOLF IN SHEEP'S CLOTHING

From behind the front line of the U.O. guards, a high-ranking official emerged, accompanied by the Captain of the Guard. Antoine Nunez was widely recognized as an advocate for minority empowerment, particularly within the military. He was being groomed for a lucrative political future. The two advanced toward a senior officer of the opposing squad—it was Shih. Pointing his finger at the officer, Nunez threatened, "Stand down—if you don't put down your weapons immediately, you will all, I repeat, *all,* be put on trial for treason. The penalty for your action here today will be death. Do I make myself clear?"

In silence, the Seals and Rangers held their ground. Again, Nunez attempted to speak, but before he could utter another word he was drowned out by the echo of his own voice rising from the theater below. Another elephant, this time bearing the South American Union flag, had begun to speak. Nunez, just like the previously humiliated officials, was projected for all to see. Frozen with indecision, his pallor suggested he was faint. But his amplified voice was strong as it bellowed throughout the arena:

"Red, yellow, black or brown... You've got to make 'em *all* feel down— like victims! We gotta keep them dependent on us as their advocates. You know, strangle out any self-esteem. Remember, once they get respect for themselves, we'll lose *our* power and influence—just like that," Nunez said, snapping his fingers to emphasize the point.

"So we've gotta shut down these do-gooders. We can't have any self-appointed saviors talking about the self-empowerment of personal responsibility, making good choices and old-fashioned self-reliance. No, no, no... We want to perpetuate the discussions and mindsets of victimhood...and the absolute, crying need for public assistance. It's always, always, always got to be everyone else's fault. All this racial equality stuff.... A *white* man's got no business having *any* conversation with *any* man of color about these topics. I mean, c'mon!"

As Nunez's mind absorbed his self-inflicted condemnation, he cried out, "This isn't fair! That was in a bar with a bunch of friends! I'd had a few too many drinks that evening. I'm just a victim in all this!" Demeaned and disgraced in everyone's eyes, he covered his ears in a childish attempt to hide from the truth. In frustration he cursed at the Seals and Rangers who continued to defy his authority. Racial prejudice had left an indelible mark on him; the bitterness of his past still dogged his steps. Disgraced before the entire world, he had actually earned a little of Hiram's sympathy. But only a little...

TOLERANCE AND CONTROL

The crowd's attention was given no reprieve as the North American elephant began to speak. This round, the spectators were voyeurs in the boardroom of the U.O. High Commission. Here, the 10 most important councilmen on earth were gathered around a conference table. Once again here was Henry Varick, the U.S. representative, speaking, "Ladies and gentlemen, we've actually managed to get a handle on controlling most of the people most of the time. The key, of course, turns out to be language. By intentionally altering and limiting the people's speech, we, in effect, silence our enemies. Lacking a viable means of expression, the people allow us to control them."

Varick looked at the other councilmen one by one as they acknowledged his conclusion. "As a matter of fact, if you recall the fable of the Tower of Babel, a supreme being achieved essentially the same results by confusing everyone's language. At the very height of their success, the mythical God came down to review their masterpiece; his response was to cast a spell and magically confuse all the languages. Thus, the people were scattered, their power broken." The mythical explanation forced laughter from some of the men seated around the table.

"Well," Jorge Weinstaut, the German representative added, " 'God' did us a favor. He showed us the way. He who controls language and communications controls the world." The camera zoomed in for a close-up as he affirmed: "We gotta be the good guys here—you know, the ones who stand for tolerance. And so, we *refuse to tolerate* any kind of speech which displays intolerance."

More laughter.

"Using this circular reasoning, we have the power to arrest and imprison practically anyone, accusing them of the hate crime of intolerance. I suppose we only want to catch the big fish in our clever nets, and then tell everyone else we are honoring the prime directive: *Tolerance must be maintained in order to guarantee peace.*"

Hearing this, the British councilman, Harold McClean, leaned back in his chair, looking up at the ceiling as he loftily mused, "Tolerance—I like the ring of it.... The way you say it, Jorge, it sounds almost holy." The group cackled even louder, waking one of the older Spanish council members, Antonio Martinez, who had dozed off during the meeting. "What was that?" he asked, trying to make sense of what little he had heard. "You say you can catch *anybody*? How do you manage that, Weinstaut?"

The German chairman responded impatiently—disrespectfully. "Tony, where have you been? Don't you know why we invest so much in our technology infrastructure—in computers and surveillance teams with listening devices? How else can we gather enough evidence to put these offenders away? Why, 25 percent of the combined revenue generated by both our daylight tax and our credit chip transaction tax has gone to pay for the electronic surveillance budget. It's what's keeping us in business! Our latest development is that new data collection operation we've got going out in the desert. Remember that 50-square-mile facility we've been talking about for *months*? Nobody can slip through our net. The only thing we haven't sacrificed for this effort is our own personal 'Special Allocation.'" The sheer mention of this vague graft prompted terse glances between the council members.

"I thought we were never supposed to talk about our extracurricular income," shot back Harold.

Each confession seemed to quicken the pace of evacuation from the VIP section.

OFFICE FOR CULTURAL ENRICHMENT

With the spectators still reeling from the last clip, the boardroom transitioned to another government office—the Office for Cultural Enrichment. It had been established to head the new government's commitment to support the arts at all levels, but in the short time the Office existed, there was no evidence that this ever happened. An attractive, middle-aged woman was seated in a large glass-enclosed office, filled with decorative furniture and walls adorned with priceless paintings. The sixth elephant, displaying the African Coalition flag, began to speak for Andrea Angelica—the Director of the Ministry for Cultural Enrichment. She seemed to be pontificating to two interns, Peter Walker and Darlene Malone.

Looking forward but addressing the woman on her right, she exclaimed cynically: "Love, love, love.... I'm sick of this love business! Crazy things happen when people start believing in 'the power of love.' Love is simply an illusion—can't they get that into their heads? What they *really* crave is *sex*—plain and simple." The other woman nodded in agreement. "We've got to keep them confused about their emotions; keep them emotionally off balance. Hit them with sexually suggestive shit day and night—you know...kinky sex, crazy stuff...the kind that messes with your mind." Darlene nodded submissively.

Peter, seated near a window, stood up and approached his superior's large oak desk. "Excuse me, Madam Director..." Andrea looked up at him, resenting the interruption. "Well, what is it?" she snapped.

"It's just that...," he paused.

"Come on—out with it. I haven't got all day!" Andrea demanded.

"Well, there are certain attitudes which pose a greater threat to social control—I mean universal pleasure—than love."

"What, for instance?" she pressed.

"Well, respect. You see..."

"Respect, hah! You show me one politician or one banker who gets any respect these days. Don't come to me with your respect."

The intern held his ground, "Think for a moment, ma'am, of the U.S. Military. There, respect is a way of life—it is a force to be reckoned with. They still have a Code of Honor. Respect is not a dead issue for them. They are willing to die for their honor. And *that*, Madam Director, poses a problem for any governmental leadership that thinks it has no need to respect anyone or anything."

As the echo of the young man's final words filled the arena, the holographic image faded away. Had Hiram and Shih accomplished their goal? Had the audience seen enough of what was behind the curtain of the Universal Order?

Could it get any worse?

CHAPTER 15

The Last Elephant Speaks

The seventh elephant, boasting the Micronesian Coalition flag, began to speak. "I tell you, Frank, this project of yours can get us all into hot water." The image jarringly shifted to a long-range shot of a structure, filling the stadium. It spanned vertically from floor to ceiling—20 stories high. This full-scale image was of the Universal Order Tower in lower Manhattan, captured by a drone from nearly a mile away. The drone's camera zoomed in on the lower section of the Tower, which housed the world's only functional quantum computer—the Mega-5.

The shot zoomed through the walls of the Tower's lower section, revealing the vast interior of the Tower's data center. Set against the Mega-5, voices continued their debate: "OK, Carl," Frank responded, "I get the point—but just *think* of it—the question of a Creator God... something that has been in doubt ever since the days of the Deists. I mean, they still believed that God had made the universe, but they doubted His power to *intervene*. And of course, that just led to more doubts. Then we discover other galaxies..." He let this word hang in the air, as if doing so would lend credence to his case. "And suddenly we're not so special anymore. Why not let the Mega-5 *tell* us whether or not there *really* is a scientific possibility that a Creator God, a supreme being, could actually exist?"

After some grumbling, Frank's colleagues accepted his suggestion. Off camera, a man chimed in, "Hey, is the digital secretary's camera turned on to catch all this?"

"The damn thing's always on, but it's easier than an intern following us around documenting everything," sneered Frank.

Frank posited his question to Mega-5 as specifically as possible: "Is there a scientific possibility that a Creator God, a supreme, omnipotent being, could actually exist?" The Mega-5 processed the entirety of human history in silent brevity. Startlingly, its electronic voice announced: "Results inconclusive—more data required."

The scene appeared to fast forward, but maintained focus on the same technicians.

"You and your bright ideas," a voice complained. "We've fed additional data into the Mega-5 for the past two years, and still no answer to your God question. M-5 keeps telling us it needs *all* the data; and we're magnitudes of order away from that! At this rate there will be no end!"

The scene changed again, but this time Frank was conspicuously absent. Carl, another employee whose first name spoke loudly on his security badge, addressed the group. "With the recent, unfortunate demise of our colleague, Dr. Frank Baumann, I regret that we must put an end to his beloved 'God Project.' Deep down, I think it was an obsession for him. But it's been six years since we asked M-5 this incredibly broad question. So in honor of Frank, I say we ask one more time. Shall we, gentlemen?" Agreement was unanimous.

Carl took a deep breath and exhaled cautiously before re-entering the question. Man's finest creation compiled and analyzed billions of variables simultaneously. He nervously twitched his fingers on the mouse to ensure the volume was up and M-5's voice response was activated. The room was incredibly quiet for a few seconds. The team seemed to be holding their breath, waiting for permission from the Mega-5 to exhale. But then it started. A soft whooshing sound like the wind could be heard, faint at first but rapidly increasing in volume. Carl tried to compensate, but the decibels continued to rise. Facial expressions throughout the room spelled out puzzled concern. The volume swell pressed on, building to an excruciating level. Everyone in the video covered their ears; soon the audience did, too. The cacophony danced through the arena, hitting an unbelievable volume, until a voice louder than thunder reverberated throughout. Words were insufficient as onlookers felt like they had touched another dimension. A sound so overwhelming, so loud, so awesome came forth from the speakers that it shattered everything else the audience had experienced that evening, climaxing with a pained murmur uttering two words: "I am." The response was unexpected. Punctuating the abhorrent whisper, one entire wall of the arena collapsed under a thunderous explosion and a blinding flash.

The entire rear section of the greatest arena in the world was suddenly vaporized and sucked out into the desert, exposing the night sky. The target had been the Control Booth. The Order would stop at nothing to conceal the truth—not only about themselves, but the ultimate truth about the universe—the *true* universal order.

As the smoke cleared, a second group of Shih's confidants emerged from cover in the American elephant. Their well-rehearsed ballet set up defensive positions and a mobile radar unit that had been stowed with them in the elephant. The equipment laid out the flight path of an incoming attack aircraft—it was about to make a second pass. In response, several mounted shoulder-launched, anti-aircraft rockets capable of neutralizing even the most sophisticated fighters blazoned. The low-flying jet fighter did not have a chance. A computer controlled launch pattern sent three rockets ablaze simultaneously, creating a vortex of three smoke trails. At their peak, all three missiles went off within milliseconds of each other, creating a debris field the jet's engines could not withstand. The jet emerged unscathed, but its trajectory shifted downward as its engines stalled.

The intentional strike on the Control Booth succeeded in interrupting the broadcast. Satellite links and hard lines immediately failed. All across the globe, millions of people who had been watching anxiously, awaited a finale—but it never came. No one outside of Las Vegas was aware that the stadium had been nearly decimated.

And then, just as it had 10 years earlier, the power grid fell—darkness descended across the civilized face of the earth. Familiar text messages went out; the world was told to wait for information around 8 p.m. the next evening. And just like before, after one night of darkness, Henry Varick reappeared on television—having aged considerably since making his original appearance 10 years earlier. Today, where once was a U.S. flag, he stood proudly in front of the Universal Order flag, surrounded by men and women of political notoriety. Among those was none other than Mei-ling. Her hair was different, her attire modest compared to her last on-screen appearance, but her beauty could not be contained.

"Ladies and gentlemen, yesterday in Las Vegas, international terrorists made a direct strike on the Theater of the Universal Order. Piloting a decommissioned fighter plane, the group made a successful missile strike on our great arena. Fortunately, *our* forces were able to knock the plane out of the air before it could do further damage, thereby saving the lives of thousands of innocent people. Unfortunately, little remains of our great arena except a burned-out shell. The terrorists responsible are the same ones who hijacked our ceremonies earlier in an attempt to deceive you with completely fabricated productions, designed solely to discredit the Universal Order. The group even used one of the show's props as a Trojan horse, but our brave soldiers were able to subdue and capture them as they emerged. Most resisted, and were killed in the ensuing firefight.

"Unfortunately, I regret to inform you that once again, they have shut down key centers of the consortium's power grid. This is but a further attempt to deceive you, the people, in the hope that you might believe the false rumor that the U.O. is an evil force at work here. Their sole objective seems to be undermining our authority.

"Their numbers have increased; their tactics have become more drastic. But do not fear, fellow citizens—we shall overcome. As before, we will stop these terrorists in their tracks. These insurgents are attempting to destroy *your* very way of life. They will stop at *nothing* to deceive us, but the truth shall prevail! The Universal Order is working tirelessly on your behalf to restore order. We will stop at nothing to maintain your safety and your security. The *one* thing we will *not* tolerate is a victory for the forces of evil. Thank you for your attention; this is the U.O. signing off."

Epilogue

And though this world with devils filled,
Should threaten to undo us,
We will not fear,
For God hath willed His truth to triumph through us.
The prince of darkness grim,
We tremble not for him;
His rage we can endure, for lo! his doom is sure;
One little word shall fell him.

—Martin Luther

Word of mouth is crucial for any author to succeed. If you enjoyed the book, please consider leaving a review where you purchased it, or on *Goodreads*, even if it's only a line or two; it would make all the difference and would be very much appreciated. You can also follow us on Twitter or "like" our page on Facebook. Thank you.

Say Hello!

WEBSITE	www.emblemmediallc.com
TWITTER	@EmblemMediaLLC
FACEBOOK	www.facebook.com/emblemmediallc
EMAIL	info@emblemmediallc.com

More from Emblem Media

THE HOUND OF HEAVEN—A MODERN ADAPTATION
by Brian and Sally Oxley & Sonja Peterson with Dr. Devin Brown

Francis Thompson's classic, *The Hound of Heaven,* is considered by many to be a poetic masterpiece. The autobiographical poem has touched lives for years and is without doubt one of the finest pieces of Christian verse ever written. This one-of-a-kind book has both the original poem, as well as a modern adaptation. Each version has a unique set of illustrations to enhance the reader's experience. Emblem Media has also produced an animated video version of the modern adaptation, which can be viewed at emblemmediallc.com. The song at the end of the video, entitled *I Finally See,* was also inspired by the poem. It is available for purchase on iTunes along with a collection of songs written and produced for Emblem Media on the CD project, *An Amazing Story.*

To stay in touch with Emblem Media for updates on *The Hound of Heaven* materials and other Emblem Media releases, please "like" us on Facebook.

WEBSITE   www.emblemmediallc.com

FACEBOOK   www.facebook.com/thehoundofheaven

Available in paperback.

THE LAST TOWER
by Brian Oxley

Imagine a sinister threat is looming, whose potential for malice is barely discernible...for now.

A series of destructive waves—shocks to the world system—takes place during the first two decades of the new millennium that initially appears to have no connection. But the ensuing shock waves do not pass and fade. They grow and converge to undermine our confidence in the entire world order.

Five friends begin to creatively imagine the results of a world dominated by a leadership with a hidden agenda. Peppering the conversation with stories that illustrate their hopes and fears, they engage in a charged dialogue. Hearts and minds confront one another to find glimmers of Truth and the unsettling possibility of supernatural involvement.

More than a prophetic fable, it's a call for some soul-searching introspection. And hey, it's just five regular guys at the Star Diner engaged in a little...spirited discussion. We're just talking...

Available on Kindle eBook and in paperback.

At the dawn of the printing press, a special kind of book rose to the top of the best-seller lists that featured a unique blend of images and text. These picture-text publications were known as Emblem books. Today, when we use the word *emblem*, we typically think of an image or object that stands for something else.

Brian Oxley's passion has always been to encourage and inspire people to a higher level of workmanship. Drawing from life experiences as a son growing up in Japan, a husband, father, and executive of a large, multinational company, he offers "food for thought" on issues regarding leadership, teamwork, and values in everyday life and business.

Through *Brian's Corner,* he shares *short* essays and stories illustrated with dramatic, original artwork...in essence, "an Emblem email." Consider this an invitation to invest a few minutes each month to reflect on some important topics in the days ahead. Please visit our website to learn more and sign up!

WEBSITE   www.brians-corner.com

TWITTER   @brianscorner

Other books by Brian Oxley

EMBLEMS OF LEADERSHIP IMAGINED—SILENT PARABLES *(Revised & Expanded)*
by Brian Oxley

This second edition of *Emblems of Leadership Imagined—Silent Parables* has been revised and expanded with seven new Emblems and eight revised Emblems along with updated content.

Using original art that conceptualizes the thoughts that are stimulated by the accompanying commentary, Brian Oxley draws the reader on a soul-searching journey for the meaning of leadership imagined. As he explains in his introduction, "We may sometimes forget that leadership is a privilege more than an entitlement. It has its rewards and acclaim, but also, at times, its heavy burdens—being accountable to customers, employees, shareholders, and our families. We need strength from the moral and spiritual realm that is greater than ourselves." Brian challenges the reader to join him in meditating on developing the effective skills needed to make an impact on the people we lead.

Available in paperback.

Coming soon from Emblem Media

LILIAS TROTTER
Documentary & Book (coming 2015)

You may have never heard of Lilias Trotter, but after seeing and reading her story, you will never forget her. Blessed with the privileged life of British aristocracy and artistic talent beyond compare, she left it all to do mission work in hostile Algeria as a single woman in the late 1800s. The beautiful journals she left behind from these difficult and dangerous years are filled with faithful insight and spectacular artwork.

We are currently in preproduction to bring this amazing woman's testimony and diaries to life through a documentary film and an artistically accurate re-creation of her journals.

BEYOND THE LOCKER ROOM
by Bret Hall & Brian Oxley

One of the significant benefits of participation in any athletic program is the life lessons of lasting value that can be learned. In this Emblem book, Bret Hall, a soccer player, and Brian Oxley, a wrestler, have teamed up to share some of the life lessons they have learned through their experiences in the athletic arena. While these lessons were learned through the grit and sweat of tough athletic competition, their impact goes far beyond the locker room. In fact, they even reach beyond the physical realm into the moral and spiritual realm, penetrating deep into the soul.

THE REFLECTING POOL
by Brian Oxley

It is said that in the moment just before your death, your entire life flashes before your eyes in an instant. In *The Reflecting Pool*, a shrewd businessman, distracted by his anger over corporate frustrations, crashes his car and now lies in a hospital bed in a deep coma hovering between life and death. His past unfolds before him in a strange dream in which his deceased father leads him back to the deep pool where, in his childhood, they would fish and talk about life. There on its crystalline surface he sees the events of his life reflected with compelling clarity, encouraging him to pursue a better future, that is, if he survives.

Made in the USA
Monee, IL
14 July 2020

36584451R00095